"de Bruler's raw, kinetic prose drives the reader deeper into a bleak world where all that glitters shines even brighter for the darkness.

The stories in *Return of the Death God* are dark, abrasive, torturous in their stark defiance of gentle convention. The characters are no less viscerally human in their pride, fear, and excess. But the words-- the words are rain to wash away the filth and quench a rasping soul."

—Paul d. Miller,
author of *Albrecht Drue, Ghostpuncher*
and *Albrecht Drue: Paranormal Dick*

For Mark Lanegan

RETURN OF THE DEATH GOD

SHORT STORIES BY CONNOR DE BRULER

MONTAG

First Montag Press E-Book and Paperback Original Edition March 2022

Montag Press ISBN: 978-1-957010-06-9
Design © 2022 Amit Dey

Montag Press Team:

Editor: Charlie Franco
Cover: Rick Febre

A Montag Press Book
www.montagpress.com
Montag Press
777 Morton Street, Unit B
San Francisco CA 94129 USA

Montag Press, the burning book with the hatchet cover, the skewed word mark and the portrayal of the long-suffering fireman mascot are trademarks of Montag Press.

Printed & Digitally Originated in the United States of America
10 9 8 7 6 5 4 3 2 1

TABLE OF CONTENTS

TRIAL RUN

It looked like a house of cards; a two-story motel just off the interstate, red doors on white frames. Each curtain-drawn window faced the on-ramp to the Fairview Road Bridge in the foothills of South Carolina. A young hustler--good-looking, no meth rot evident in her face--left the room with a 7-Up bottle in her hand.

Luanne snapped a few pics through the gap in the steering wheel with the P900.

Vaquero got antsy and lit up a Camel Crush. She was hungover and couldn't handle the smell.

"Put it out," she said.

V cracked the tinted window and tossed out the cig.

"That ain't Sprite or Mountain Dew she carrying," he said.

"No, it's 7-Up."

He scoffed.

"You'd think we was in Houston how much lean this guy peddles in a day."

"Why? They like the drank out in Texas?"

"Where you been at? It's the Third Ward all day."

"They got wards out there like in New Orleans?"

"You ain't been?"

"To Texas? Never."

"You missin' out."

"On what? More humidity?"

The girl stood at the edge of the street and leaned against a splintered, tar-covered telephone pole.

She snapped another pic with the Nikon.

"How come you take so many photos of random shit?"

"Keep the client happy. Remind him I'm not wasting his time."

"Bunch of garbage photos isn't admissible in court."

She laughed.

"Nobody's goin' the court with this stuff. Half my shit doesn't even go to a lawyer. This is the minor leagues, kid. Last year I had a client who killed his husband. A month before that, a runaway outbid her mother for me *not* to find her."

"Shit," he said. "*His* husband?"

"That's all you got out of that?"

A red jeep pulled into the parking lot and cruised up beside the telephone pole. She snapped photos of the exchange. The buyer handed the girl the money and a fresh bottle of real soda.

"That's clever," V said. "So you don't see her without a drink in her hand."

She snapped a final pic and puts away the camera.

"Is that who I think it is in the car?"

V reached for the binoculars.

"Back seat. Smokin' a Black and Mild. That's her."

Luanne started the engine and took a swig of her coffee and then chased it with a belt of Gatorade.

"You sure you don't want me to drive?"

"I'm sure," Luanne said.

The tires crunched across the gravel as they followed the red jeep along the street and onto the highway bridge. She allowed a minivan to merge ahead of her.

"Don't lose him."

"I can still see him."

The jeep took the first exit onto a secluded backroad through the bright sun-splashed foliage and she followed.

"You're getting awful close," V said.

"Everyone rides each other's ass on these little country roads. You hang back thirty yards you end up looking suspicious."

"I don't know," he said and placed another cig between his lips without lighting it.

"Get out my camera and get their license plate."

He took the Nikon and snapped the plate.

"Better not be blurry."

He snapped the plate again to make sure.

"How's that one look?"

"I don't know how to work this thing," he said, tapping menu options.

"Don't worry about it."

She took another sip of her coffee.

The red jeep pulled onto an isolated property overlooking a scum-covered pond that might have had alligators back in the 1960s before nature was beaten into submission and scarcity became its main attribute.

Luanne floored the gas as soon as the jeep turned as if she had somewhere to be. She parked out of sight on a patch of high dogfennel and killed the engine.

"I'm gonna smoke a cigarette," V said, unbuckling his seatbelt. He stepped out into the weeds, slamming the door behind him.

She reached into the glove compartment and took out the Ruger LCP and the half-pint of vodka. She unscrewed the cap and took a swig.

It started with a call around nine o'clock in the morning; still too early to think. She sat on her swivel chair in the dark corner of her apartment dining room, a blank excel sheet on the four-year-old laptop screen in front of her. After reaching for the liquor cabinet, she threw a liberal splash of bourbon into her coffee. The cell phone vibrated across the desk. She caught it before it dropped off the side and answered it.

It was another missing girl. Another case where drugs figured heavily into the decision-making of the mark. The client was male and sounded down-to-earth and more than comfortable talking to a private investigator like it had happened before. His name was Bill Tycho. He was an ex-redneck millionaire with a contracting firm that built golf club mansions across the state. His daughter was an underage prostitute and oxy user. Seventeen years old.

"So what's the problem? You can't afford rehab, a little spot out in Missouri where she can suck off twenty-year-olds and pet horses?"

"Last rehab I sent her to in Florida almost killed her. We're gonna try an outpatient program this time under my roof. No horses. No other junkies."

"You know my rates?"

"I do. And if you jerk me around on this and bleed the clock without bringing her back, I'll make it hard for you to spend my money."

"I'm gonna have to stop you there," she said. "I can tell you where she is. I can't bring anyone to you."

He paused.

"How about triple the rate?"

The SOB knew her weakness was money. That's why he found her and not some seasoned ex-cop with a law degree. He needed a lowlife to do his dirty work. If she was going to take somebody in, she'd need a partner. That's where V came in.

She met V back in Greenville at her ex-boyfriend's place. A bald, security-guard type had kicked in the door to the apartment the same night she was tossing the place for the eight-hundred he still owed her. Her ex was a low-level weed and shroom dealer with a gallery of sketchy friends he allowed in and around the apartment from noon to midnight. For anyone looking to find deadbeats south of Earl Street, his crash pad was the main stop. The bald guy must have seen her silhouette in the window. When he kicked in the door, he demanded that she tell him where V was. He called him by his last name: Lawful. The irony wasn't lost on him.

Luanne was in the middle of robbing her ex, pulling the wrinkled bills from a hiding space beneath the upturned couch.

"You're a bounty hunter. State law says a private citizen doesn't have to tell you anything."

"What are you doing here anyway?"

Again, she recited state and federal law.

"Is he hiding here?"

She showed the bounty hunter the stolen cash and the ransacked state of the apartment.

"Does it look like I live here?" she said, pointing to her crowbar beside the window.

He holstered his sidearm.

"You got a mouth on you, bitch."

She counted out eight-hundred dollars and stuffed it in her wallet.

"I got what I came for. You can knock yourself out and wait for whoever."

She attempted to slide past him.

He blocked the door frame.

"You ain't going nowhere."

He pushed her against the wall and closed the door with his foot. His face was inches from hers.

"You think you can stand here and make a fool out of me."

She struggled.

He put his hand over her mouth and wrestled her to the floor.

She tried to kick his groin but he pinned her legs with his knees. He brought all of his weight down on her as she screamed.

A shadow moved across the wall and crowded the entranceway. With a swift knock of the crowbar, the bounty hunter was out cold.

She would later tell the prosecutor that the bounty hunter, Eric Currman, would have likely raped her that night had Vaquero Lawful not saved her. Her testimony didn't help him much and he went to state prison on a five-year sentence anyway.

They cut him loose after two. Overcrowding.

She drove down to the state capital and caught him outside the prison with her business proposition.

V didn't have anywhere else to go except for the bus stop.

"Not everyday a white lady offers you a ride and a meal while talking about making *you* money. Especially not the day you get out of prison," she said as they drove north on the highway.

"You wouldn't know how things turn out for me," V said.

She took him to a diner and bought him a cup of coffee and a plate of pancakes and told him about the job and offered him a flat rate.

"It doesn't sound at all legal," he said. "And I just got out of prison."

"It's not like we're gonna pimp her out or hold her for ransom. Her dad wants to help her out. She's a minor. He has a right to get her back."

"If he's going through you then he's hiding something," V said. "And I ain't worried about the morality factor. I'm worried about the fuckin' legality factor. I just got out. Five minutes ago."

She bit off a piece of bacon.

"Yeah, you're right. You just got out. You got no place. No money. No job. You know? You saved my life so I thought I'd cut you in on this thing and get you started. A thousand bucks might get you out of the South at least."

"A thousand bucks? Maybe. And how much you makin'? Three? Four?"

"I'm making what I'm making. We're talking about you."

"We're talking about what I can do for you," he said. "We're talking about this being a potential trial run for a longer partnership."

"I'm not hiring a partner," she said.

"You're hiring me for a single job. That's like hiring a partner. We'll call it a trial run. What's a thousand dollars gonna do for me? Huh? Might get me as far as Washington D.C. where I can freeze to death on the street. I don't need to get out of the South. What I need is an opportunity and what you need is a sober person to do the heavy lifting. Am I right?"

She smirked and leaned back in the booth.

"Am I that bad?"

"Nah, you hold it together ok. But I'm trained for this. My pops was an alcoholic."

She paused for a moment.

"Alright. A thousand flat and a trial run to go into business together."

They shook hands.

V didn't see her swig the Vodka, but he did see her stuff the miniature pistol into her back pocket.

He blew mentholated smoke toward the trees.

"You got you a throwaway?"

"Just in case," she said, locking the car.

"The hell? Keep the door open."

"I got equipment in there. I don't want it open."

He tapped his ash into the weeds.

"What if one of us has to get inside in a split second and you got the key in your pocket?"

"You ever done anything like this before?"

"I'm just giving you a for instance. Look where we are, who is gonna steal your camera out here. They can't even see in the car with your tint job."

She took out the key and unlocked the doors.

"You ready for this?"

"Sure," she said.

V threw his cig onto the road and they approached. The property was tucked back into the cooler woods behind a narrow, cleanly-paved driveway. The house might have looked nice a few years ago, a modest vacation spot in the country, but the active rot of the opiate life had worn the place down: beer cans in the uncut lawn, a sweet chemical smell from the padlocked shed, foundational beams shot up by a .22 rifle.

"This is some Chainsaw Massacre bullshit," V said. "This guy has guns. You know it'll be crazy firepower. And all you got is a pea shooter the size of a burner phone."

".380 ACP can still kill a man outright."

"I don't know what that is."

"The caliber of the bullet," she said.

They surveyed the house for a few minutes and tried to see beyond the windows. The place was dead quiet. Luanne stepped to the back porch and looked through the mosquito screen. The kitchen was a mess, of course. The TV was still on; internet porn looped on a laptop playlist and linked by an aux cord. The sound was off. She took out a credit card and unlatched the screen door. The second door, the glass door to the kitchen, was unlocked and she stepped inside. Moving fast, she entered the hallway and saw the girl splayed out on the bed, still clothed, a cup of dirty soda on the nightstand. The girl caught a glimpse of Luanne in the hallway through her promethazine haze and did nothing. She just stared at the ceiling. A toilet flushed in the bathroom.

She retreated around the corner as the older man walked into the hall. She winced. She had no plan. The man inched toward the corner.

The girl laughed.

He looked back.

"The fuck you laughin' at?"

Luanne stood behind him and drew the pocket pistol.

He stopped dead as she pressed the barrel to his neck.

"Don't move. Don't say a word."

"You here from Cantrell?"

"Interlock your fingers on the top of your head," she said. "I'm not a drug dealer and I'm not here to rob you."

"Then what the fuck are you doing in my house?"

"Get on your knees."

He ducked low and rammed his shoulder into her stomach. She dropped to the floor, firing a shot at the ceiling.

Just like old times, V jumped in at the last minute and incapacitates him with a right hook.

"You trying to get someone killed?"

"I...don't know what to say," she said.

"You're still drunk aren't you?"

"I'm a PI, not a kidnapper," she said. "Come on, get the girl, and let's go."

V walked into the bedroom and threw the girl over his shoulder. They ran out of the house and into the foliage toward the parked car. The girl didn't fight back.

"Where are we going?"

"You're cleaning up," Luanne said.

"Yay, sobriety," the girl said sarcastically.

They pushed through the rhododendrons' branches and hustled over to the car. She opened the backdoor for V and he sets the girl inside.

"Get in the back with her."

"I know what I'm doing," V said.

She ran around the driver's seat and started the engine. The dark sedan peeled out of the weed patch and down the narrow country road. She chugged her coffee as she drove.

The girl started to laugh.

"What all are you on right now?" V said.

"Don't engage," Luanne said, glancing at them through the rearview mirror.

"It's cool."

Luanne pulled her cell phone out of her jeans and dialed the client's number. Driving with one hand, she waited as the cell rang for a full minute. The contractor finally answered.

"Yeah?"

"We got her," she said. "We're coming to you."

"I'm on a job. I'll text you the address."

When the text came through, she handed the phone to V. "Put that into the GPS."

The girl laughed the whole way to the building site.

She slowed the car as they approached.

"Where are we going?" the girl said.

"We're taking you to your dad," V said.

She peered through the windshield.

"That ain't my dad."

V said nothing.

Luanne glanced at him through the rearview.

"Don't say anything," she said. "Let's just get paid."

V looked at the girl.

Big Bill Tycho waited for them beside his white pickup with his arms crossed. His employees loitered around the frame of the house, smoking, spitting seeds, and drinking from their water bottles. Luanne parked the sedan sideways across a patch of raw clay.

Two of his enforcers opened up the back seat and pulled out the girl. V stepped out after her and another man patted him down. The same man frisked Luanne and she showed him the Ruger. Tycho didn't say anything. The girl was inside the back of the white truck.

"Well, you outdid my expectations. I'll put in a good word for you."

Luanne kept staring at V who didn't say a word.

"I guess you want to get paid then?"

"That's usually how this works," she said.

He reached into his dark khakis and took out a bank envelope.

"Here, count it. I won't be offended."

V wiped his brow with his shirt.

"So who is the girl anyway? If she isn't your kid?"

"Shut up," Luanne said.

"I'm just askin'. I wanna know what I did this for."

Tycho looked at Luanne.

"Who is this guy anyway? Your muscle?"

"You don't need to worry about it. We're paid, so we don't care who she is," she said, and gave V a look.

V kept his eyes on Tycho.

The men around them went silent and circled the sedan.

Luanne counted the money.

"We're good," she said. "Let's go."

A man with a white hard hat sat down on the hood of the sedan.

"You didn't say you were gonna have a partner on this," Tycho said.

"I needed to make sure it got done right."

"That wasn't part of the contract."

"What's the difference? It's the same amount of money."

Bill Tycho winced and adjusted his belt.

"What's the difference? I paid you for discretion. Now I got another guy in the mix."

"He'll keep his mouth shut."

"It don't sound like he's keeping his mouth shut to me," he said and turned to one of his employees. "Dale, this man sound like he's keeping his mouth shut to you?"

He shook his head.

"No, sir. Sound to me like he's asking a bunch of questions."

V kept his eyes moving as they argued. He stared at the passed-out girl in the back of Tycho's truck, at the worker sitting on the hood of the car, at Dale as he smiled and stared back into his eyes.

Luanne acted like she was stuffing the envelope in her back pocket as she reached for the Ruger.

A hefty man to her right reached into his toolbox for a jet black .357 magnum.

She drew the pocket Ruger and fired.

Bill Tycho dropped to his knees with a bullet to the gut.

V lunged for the nearest man and tackled him to the red clay.

The magnum's report echoed through the site.

Two of them pulled V away by his arms.

Luanne fired again. The bullet glanced off an exposed septic tank and pierced the passenger window of Tycho's truck and the girl was dead.

HOUSE CALL

On the phone, she said, "When you reach the apartment, just follow my tears," but it was a trail of soapy water that led him down the narrow hall. He was careful as he followed the translucent beads. He sidestepped the thicker ones and walked slowly so the little domes of liquid wouldn't shift and absorb into the green wood panels. The bedroom door was open and he could see through to the master bathroom (its heavy black door also precariously ajar) where his blurred reflection stared back at him through the mirror's filter of condensation.

The clerical collar was tight around his unshaven neck. He scratched at his three-day accumulation of stubble. Wearing his long black cassock, he looked both out of place and, strangely, as if he belonged here in this darkened apartment, which appeared to have been furnished for a singular kind of oblique mood. It was as if he had become the subject of a disturbing oil-painting. What would he have called it? Something like *The Last Rights of Maria Ramos-Mendoza*. That was the name she had given him on the phone. Perhaps she was an artist. Her voice was cold, mechanical. She told him she was an atheist, but she had no alternate explanation for the haunting in the apartment, that a diabolic entity had taken root in the unit, that she was being driven to insanity, that she was being watched, that she needed him tonight. Most of the people he exploited were Latino immigrants. Her name raised no suspicion. But why assert her atheism?

Nothing here was right.

The clergyman angle had been his side hustle for eight long years. The gypsy cat burglars called him The Father. Most days he went by Jack. House calls were his MO. He used high-grade burner phones and a Lithuanian rerouting app to scalp calls from the diocese. Advertising himself was too risky. He only ran the short game. The payouts were often meager and when those who were spiritually afflicted didn't make a sizable donation to the parish, he'd have to hit the same spot for the electronics and gold and silver after rigging an entry point.

The building hadn't looked wrong to him, just another vertical tower covered in rickety fire escapes with a gutter-like moat of an alleyway jammed within the crowded downtown. The lobby walls were a vague yellow: the color of aging plastic. The apartment was fourteen flights up. The front door opened on its own after he knocked.

He sat on the edge of the bed as he stared into the bathroom. She was naked on the floor of the standing shower, hot water still running. He thought it was suicide at first. Sure, call up the holy man, get somebody to find her body. But her throat had been slashed wide open. Nobody checked out like that. It wasn't a clean job either, the kind done with a razor in one stroke. Somebody had cut deep and practically removed her jugular. Blood ran down her chest and stomach and pooled around the edges of the drain between her legs.

The cellphone on the nightstand rang. The rose gold iPhone vibrated across the shellacked surface and fell to the floor.

He backed out of the room and through the hall. The photographs and watercolors she had framed along the way looked hideous to him now.

He passed into the stairwell and didn't bother to grip the knob with his sleeve to close the front door.

The neighbors were fighting a few doors away. The fight carried through the walls. At least one was fighting while the other kept screaming. The walls were thin.

Jack's path was blocked. The professional was descending the upper steps cleaning a short fillet blade with a dark-blue bandanna. Everything else about his clothing was black from his disposable shoe covers to his powderless latex gloves, even the stocking cap around his scalp. He finished cleaning the blade and pocketed the bandanna.

"Evening, Reverend," he said.

His face was exposed, but Jack didn't recognize him.

"Evenin'," he said.

"Why don't you step back inside the apartment and we'll talk?"

He gestured with the knife.

Jack shrugged.

"I think there's been a misunderstanding. I'm not a Reverend."

"I don't care what you are."

These kinds of hired guys, usually ex-police or ex-military, were like the plague to a con artist. Most of them rarely spoke. He didn't like how much this one had to say. Talkers were usually sadists.

He came a few steps closer with only the knife in hand.

"Get back in there."

He let his head drop in defeat.

"Okay," he said, reaching into the hollowed pocket of his cassock to unholster the Sig Sauer he had strapped to his back. He drew the P938 and pulled the trigger. The spent cartridge danced along the floor like a loose bottle cap. The professional's knees buckled before he fell down the concrete steps. There was no blood, just smoke and the ring of tinnitus.

The son of a bitch wore a vest. The professional drew his own pistol from an ankle holster and fired back along the incline of the steps.

Jack stood in a haze of plaster dust. The building's foundation seemed to shudder amid the sporadic gunfire. He retreated into the unit and slammed the entrance shut. He started to work the many chains and bolts affixed to the doorsill when a single shot burst the peephole and grazed his shoulder. Hot glass from the lens in the door singed his face. He hit the floor and crawled down the hall, passing the bedroom until he could roll sideways into the kitchenette.

The hitman stopped shooting. He was hurt from the bullet to the vest and he was getting sloppy. Jack could hear the man's back as it slid down the door. He listened as he snapped open the breech with an audible click and rattled loose the spent casings from the cylinder.

Jack glanced across the kitchenette to the window above the sink. He could see the grimy metal of the fire escape. His shoulder was bleeding. He pulled a long towel down from the handle of the stove and tied it as best he could around his shoulder and beneath his armpit. He pressed the magazine release and counted his rounds. Four left. One ready to go in the chamber. Had he only fired one shot? He had no backup magazine.

The hired gun outside the door was finished loading and blew out the main lock, kicking his way in as the rest of the chains gave way. He could hear him storm down the hall and clear the bedroom. When the bedroom was clear, he made his way, even slower, toward the miniature kitchen.

Jack crouched low and crept from the center of the room to the edge of the open doorway.

"What kind of a fuckin' priest carries a gun?"

His steps were moving the green boards of the hallway as he drew closer.

Jack made sure to stay low and aimed upward.

The floorboards of the hall creaked.

The hitman hadn't yet turned the corner.

Jack's finger was heavy on the trigger.

The phone in the bedroom started ringing again.

He could hear him retrace his steps to the bedroom and search for the phone.

Jack took his chance and pulled open the locks on the window. He tried to force it open but the frame was fused to the sill. He ran to the next room, a small living area, and hid behind a lone bookcase.

The professional entered the small kitchen and walked into the living area with the loaded revolver in both hands. He checked the back of the couch.

From behind the slender bookcase, Jack aimed at the back of his knee, then raised his aim to the man's hand. He pulled the trigger and the black latex glove which held the pistol shattered in a mist of red. The pistol was expelled from the stump of his hand and bounced from the couch cushion to the floor below the coffee table. Jack took another shot at his knee and missed. The bullet entered the hitman's thigh and he fell against the wall.

Jack kept the gun on him.

The professional knew what kind of wound he was facing and kept his good hand on his thigh.

"What the fuck kind of priest are you?"

"I'm not a priest," he said. "I'm just a conman in a costume who was in the wrong place at the wrong time."

"Shit."

Blood was welling up between his fingers as he pressed on the wound. A steady flow of blood drained from the tangle of latex and flesh above his wrist as well.

"Shit," he said again, his face rapidly losing color. "I'm gonna die in this girl's apartment."

Jack aimed between his wincing eyes.

"You wanna go slow and think about things, or do you want a headshot and just be done with it?"

"I wasn't supposed to die here. Not for that dumb son of a bitch. I was supposed to kill the girl and get paid and disappear. Everyone's gonna know who I am and what I did."

"There's no use reflecting," Jack said, steadying his shot.

"Wait. Don't shoot. Don't you wanna know why?"

"Not really."

"I can make you pretty rich though."

"How?"

"Senator Rick Graham. Third District. State. He used to keep her on the side until she was threatening to go to the press. He's been trying to get this bitch to kill herself for a year. He's been sending calls, getting the power shut off in the building, staging things on the fire escape to look like something leering back at her. He's even poisoned her food so she's seeing things. She's got mental problems. We thought all she needed was a nudge to get her on a ledge. But she wouldn't do it. She wouldn't take herself out as he wanted. So, I was gonna make it look like a cartel murder or a serial killer. He was desperate."

"But tonight, she called the wrong kind of priest."

"I'm telling you. You can ruin this guy's life. He will pay you whatever you want. Especially, since my cut's off the table."

"I try not to underestimate desperate men with a lot of power. He'll probably just send someone else like you."

"I'm the only guy who knows about this. It was between him and me. That's why he thought he could get away with it."

"And who exactly are you?"

"Just a mercenary who did his time in the desert and did what I did to support a habit."

"In that case, thank you for your service," Jack said and pulled the trigger.

His head disintegrated. An unrecognizable mass of bloody tissue and white skull fragments oozed down the crude plaster into a puddle at Jack's feet. He checked the headless body's pockets for a cellphone and found an antiquated Samsung burner. He had no wallet, but he did manage to find a money clip with six hundred dollars wrapped around a half-baggy of black tar smack. He discarded the heroin and pocketed the little score. It was more than he might have made on a typical house call.

He holstered the P938 and opened the long window, stepping onto the fire escape. It was beginning to rain. He gripped the jagged railing and let the rain fall on his face to hopefully wash away the blood that had splattered. He kept his eyes on the windows of the adjacent buildings. There was no one that he could easily see watching him. He picked up his pace. He knew he was going to lay low until the heat blew over, but he wasn't sure if he would blackmail the senator. Depending on how much he could gouge the prick for, he could be looking at a potential retirement.

He heard sirens in the distance and his heart raced. He skipped a step and the sole of his shoe caught the fabric of his cassock. A crisp sliver of rust broke off the rail and he fell forward over the barrier. His body turned one hundred and eighty degrees in free fall. He felt the brief sensation of being cradled by the wind. Lights flashed around him, and his body crushed the hood of the police cruiser.

GHOST DANCE

The best advice I got at the Silver-Dollar was not to perform a McDance, a faux-sexy tease set to some radio staple. If I wanted to make money, I had to market myself, give the gawkers something they couldn't get from the other girls. Another dancer had cornered the goth angle. She wore black lingerie and danced to music like The Kills and Rob Zombie. A Latina girl danced to *reggaeton* and the occasional *corrido*. Two former cheerleaders and an ex-Hooters girl had monopolized hip-hop. Denise, an expert ass-clapper from Memphis, suggested I dance to country music. She told me to wear a confederate flag bikini top and cut-off jeans. I could play with a red MAGA hat and toss it into the crowd. I said if I were going to do that, I might as well strip in an SS uniform and dance to *Flight of the Valkyries*.

I never really had much of a persona there. I lost a lot of money paying the off-stage fee to venture beyond the tip rail. I thought there might be money out there; shy guys who need attention, somebody to listen. I didn't understand a small club like the Silver-Dollar, a one-level stucco building on the edge of the freeway, didn't attract any real high-rollers. Some nice guys spent a little, but most of the guys in the back were total rocks. No tips. No lapdances. We had minimal protection since our only bird-dog besides the DJ and the owner was getting old. A rock followed a dancer to her car one night. A week later, two men shot each other in the guest parking lot over a bag of dope.

I landed an audition at the only 7-up factory in the region sixty miles north on the interstate: a place called The Julep Cup. There, I managed to carve out a niche. It was some kind of old-Hollywood, glamour aesthetic. I danced to a lot of P.J. Harvey, the B-52s, Mr. Bungle's *Pink Cigarette*, even some of Beck's tracks from *Midnight Vultures*. Denise, who had taken me under her wing since I started, stole eighty bucks and my Kate Spade bag my last night at the old club. My father had given me that bag for graduating high school a month before he gave up on trying to kick oxy and drove out to the Blue Ridge Parkway to take his own life. Denise didn't know that. She felt betrayed, but I was too upset to ever forgive her.

The Julep Cup had an ethical house and off-stage fee, but I wasn't making near what the other girls made my first two weeks. The girls at The Julep Cup were chameleons. They didn't sell themselves, they sold the ambiance of the club as if they were spawned from the same material as the uphol-stery and wall lining. Their game was more about being in the right place at the right time with mathematical precision rather than an old-fashioned hustle. This place was in the fast lane. I had no sensei. No guidance. These girls were all veterans with IRAs who paid their rent and childcare bills on time. I dialed back the persona but kept the song list and started flirting with most of the newcomers. I went for the reserved types who maybe wanted to talk about their day or current events. I gave the stingy ones my sob stories, keeping them short and believable. The first night I made any real money, a group of Bangladeshi engineers came in to celebrate. The younger ones were terrified. They didn't look old enough to drink. I installed myself as their unofficial strip club etiquette coach. I paid my rent and the seventy-five-dollar late fee the next day. I kept working there and learned to keep up. I got friendly with a few bird-dogs. The doorman's wife was a baker and brought us cookies and cupcakes a few times which the girls threw in the trash, or ate in front of her to be polite before purging in the bathroom. My aesthetic didn't attract the same kind of patron each time. I had no specific types. A lot of older men preferred to watch me dance from a distance. Only younger, foreign men wanted to have a drink with me. Frat guys and sports bar-type guys bought lapdances.

Six months into working steady, I started getting a civilian. Civilians are other girls, customers not peelers. Girls came in groups most of the time, loud, obnoxious groups. Not this lady. The loners were lesbians. I don't care for women, but I never cared for any of the men I danced for either. Dancing for a woman was a nice break from the creepy looks and perverted questions. I became this woman's all-time favorite. She had lunch there once a week and bolstered my Friday night revenue. She didn't ask for my name like a lot of the guys when she first bought a lapdance. I told her my name was Garland, like Judy Garland. She gave me her full name, Vandy Fisk. It sounded made-up, but she didn't sound like she was kidding. I followed up with the usual chit-chat and asked if she was from around here.

"No," she said. "I'm from Montana."

"All the way from Montana?"

She nodded.

I kept playing the part. I asked her if she liked girls. The follow up was to say that I liked girls too. Maybe she'd give me a ten-spot or a twenty right there. Instead, she said, "No, I don't" in a flat, matter-of-fact tone that killed my next line. Then she said, "There's something about you that interests me."

So, *that* was her fantasy. We were playing the latent game. She wanted to pretend she was only dipping a toe in the same pond. I shifted gears and told her I usually didn't dance for women but something drew me to her. That was a good line. That was twenty-dollar-tip flirting, but I only got another five once our time was up.

The next time I saw her, she was standing in the parking lot smoking a cigarette. My shift was over. She was waiting for me. My stomach churned. Of all the creeps I had dealt with, I didn't give Vandy a second thought. She didn't smile when she saw me, she just handed me a wad of cash.

"Can I pay for some of your time?"

"I don't see people outside the club," I said.

"I'm not paying for your stripper persona. I'm paying you."

"I don't do that kind of thing."

"I'm not trying to buy sex," she said. "I'm a private investigator. I wanna talk to you."

"What do you wanna talk to me for?"

"You're not in trouble. You might know some things that could help me find someone."

I asked her if I could see some proof.

"Sure," she said as she set the cigarette in the corner of her lips and handed me a leather cred case. Both her driver's license and her PI license were issued from Montana and her real name was Vandy Fisk. I handed her back the case.

"This isn't issued for North Carolina," I said.

"No, it isn't. That's why I need your help. Under your state's law, I only have a thirty-day window to investigate before I'm operating illegally."

"How many days do you have left?"

"Ten," she said. "I'll buy dinner. We can talk in public."

I shrugged.

"I'll follow you in my car," I said.

I told her I thought I was the one playing her, but she was playing me.

"You're good at what you do," she said. "My daughter was a stripper."

"She stopped?"

"She's dead," Vandy said as she pulled out a notebook from a portfolio.

She had taken me to a lonely diner in the center of town where the booths were fake leather and the kitchen grease condensed on the ceiling tile. The server made it clear with her expression that she didn't approve of lesbians. I was wearing my gray hoodie and expensive leggings. Vandy was wearing jeans and a dark blue windbreaker.

"I'm sorry," I said. "I know what that's like."

"Yeah? That's too bad. You know, I took this assignment and came all this way because I know where my client is coming from. The girl I'm looking for is a lot like my daughter."

The server brought Vandy a cup of half-caf and my Miller High-Life. She told me I could get anything I wanted, so I ordered an omelet and some toast. When the old bitch was gone, I asked Vandy why she singled me out. She paused for a second then told me nobody from the Silver-Dollar would talk.

"How do you know I worked there?"

"A girl let it slip. Seemed pissed off you left that club."

I rolled my eyes.

"That bitch thinks I owe her."

"Makes more sense to me that a person would talk more about a place if they didn't have to worry about keeping their job."

"It's been a minute since I worked there."

She showed me a glossy photo printed off Facebook.

"Do you recognize this girl?"

I studied the face. I didn't recognize her at first. I felt bad about it and kept staring at the photo. This dark girl wasn't wearing any makeup. It was hard to picture her at the club. I still wasn't certain when I gave Vandy a name.

"I think that might be Selena."

"That's the name she went by?"

"Yeah," I said. "She was Latina."

"How do you know?"

"She danced to Mexican and Puerto Rican music for all the road and construction guys."

Vandy wrote everything down. She had pretty handwriting.

"Did you hear her speak Spanish?"

"Not really. I assumed she could," I said.

"Did she ever speak it with the Hispanic clientele?"

"We don't listen to each other's conversations in the club. We're too busy hustling ourselves. The music's too fuckin' loud anyway."

"Right," she said. "Maybe she talked about where she was from?"

"Girls at the Silver-Dollar don't talk like that. Everybody has a right to their secrets. Some do private parties, some do drugs, some escort, some have pimps. You don't ask about that kind of shit. It isn't a sisterhood. Every other girl on the pole is your direct competition."

"Noted," she said.

"These questions are weird."

"Everything helps," she said looking down at her notepad.

I drained the beer in front of me.

"Are you certain this is her?"

I shook my head.

"It's hard to tell without the makeup. Her hair was lighter than that."

"Here," she said and started scrolling through her iPhone. She showed me another picture, a selfie.

"Oh, shit. That's her," I said. "That's Selena."

"You're sure this time?"

"Definitely, she had a tattoo of a dreamcatcher on her hip."

"That's who I'm looking for. Good. Did she have any regulars?"

"No," I said. "Nobody liked her like an all-time favorite, but she got followed to her car once."

"Do you know who?"

"Fuck yeah, I do. That was Gorgeous George."

I couldn't believe I had forgotten about Gorgeous George.

"Pretty boy?"

"We just called him that 'cause he was gross. He was this big old creep. They said he had her by the throat before the bouncer got to him."

"Can you describe him to me?"

"He's white. Overweight. Thin mustache. Scruffy. Ear hair. Dracula widow's peak. Smelled like BO and cheap cigs."

"Do you remember his real name?"

"I don't," I said.

"He get banned from the club?"

"He better have. Didn't see him again. I hope he went to jail."

"Do you know if Selena pressed charges?"

"No, I never saw either of them after that. Is that when she went missing?"

Vandy shook her head.

"I wouldn't be here if that were the case. Your old coworker was already a missing person by the time any of this happened."

"She's from Montana?"

Vandy nodded.

I got my omelet and started eating my toast first. She thanked me for the information and gave me her card if I thought of anything else. She paid the check and left me alone in the diner.

On my drive home, I tried to remember more about that weirdo we called Gorgeous George. I was sitting in my living room with my makeup remover when I thought of something and called Vandy.

"Hello?" she said on the other end of the phone.

"It's me, Garland."

"That was fast."

"I forgot to tell you something about that guy."

"Hold on, let me get my pad."

I waited.

"Alright, go ahead."

"He had a Looney-Toons vibe."

"He was crazy?"

"No, no. Like a perverted Looney-Toons thing. He was into them big time. He drew Daffy Duck and Bugs Bunry on bar napkins and gave them to the girls."

"You're joking. Could he draw well?"

"They were great. They looked like real cartoons. And if he got a good look at your crotch he'd say 'I thought I taw a putty cat' in the Tweety Bird voice."

"That's perfect. Can you think of anything else?"

"That's all I got for now," I said.

"You don't know how much you helped me out," she said. "You can call me anytime if you remember anything. It doesn't matter how trivial."

"Hey, do I get to know what's going on?"

"I can't do that right now," she said. "It wouldn't be right."
I had assumed as much and let it go.

Ten days passed. I checked my phone after every dance, between each meal, sometimes in the middle of the night. I drove myself to tears trying to recall new details, to absorb the knowledge from the collective ether. I couldn't let it go. I couldn't relax. I couldn't focus on making money. Had I caught whatever fueled Vandy? Touched by the same virus? What did I care? I barely knew Selena. I didn't even know her real name. I had started something and didn't know how to stop. I became desperate for some kind of closure to release me. Working at the club became unbearable with the distraction. Every rumor I had ever heard in passing now dogged me like an opiate craving. Every man became a ghost and every dancer was a reflection of the same image while I suffocated behind glass.

I half-expected this strange anxiety to die off on the eleventh day, then I knew it was over. I could only think of Vandy in terms of fleeting images. Over time, her features warped in my memory and began to fuse with other civilians that I began to see around the club. I imagined her getting on the plane and going back to wherever she came from in Big Sky Country, empty-handed. But Selena's face never changed.

The fever subsided and I got my focus back as I continued to work the club. The experience stayed with me. The missing girl and the out-of-state PI on the hunt lost their urgency and became another part of my growing collection of stories. It was far from the worst thing to ever happen to me, but it was, up to that point, the most interesting. Every night at the club was worth a conversation. I started writing everything down on my mornings and days off. It felt like the only way to separate these things from myself, to stop carrying them around. I used to wake up in the morning already crushed under the pressure of what might come; the looks, the comments, the groping, the haggling, the complaining, the requests. Sometimes I would write a few sentences, sometimes a few pages, and then it was gone. I was no longer a receptacle for these experiences, they were just passing through me.

I had a few good nights that next month. A sixty-year-old car dealership owner asked me and another dancer to hang on his shoulders in the champagne room while he threw a party for some Florida investors. A group of Japanese businessmen stormed the club until closing the following week. The same weekend, I had a college student thrown out for trying to lick my breast.

On a Thursday afternoon, I was dancing for the only four guys in the club. They were all in their early to late thirties, all in business casual attire, and they didn't appear to be together. I danced to a standard lounge classic, slow and seductive. Just one guy was paying attention. He was the youngest looking of the group. He wore a red polo shirt and khakis. He tipped me a few dollars and clapped when I was finished. I gathered up what little money had been thrown on stage. While I was doing my best to scoop it all up, he took his napkin out from under his beer and wrote something down. It looked like he had already started writing it while I was dancing. He finished it quickly and folded it before hooking it into my g-string. I hated it when guys did that. Now and then, men would sneak business cards or religious pamphlets into a stack of cash. My adrenaline raced every time I saw a guy doing it since thinking about Gorgeous George. I got to the back and straightened up my money, then pulled the folded napkin from my hip. It was only a phone number and a short note that said, "Great set." Pimps and human traffickers frequented clubs trying to earn the girls' trust. I threw the note in the trash. Things started to pick up at around eight o'clock. I had a shot of tequila with an old black man who said he was from Detroit and moved down South to be closer to his sons. I gave a private table dance for a young man who was afraid to smile because of his bad teeth. Toward the end of the night, I was in the dressing room considering paying the house and DJ fee to go home early. One of the veteran dancers was sorting out her locker, talking trash with two other girls. I wasn't listening until I caught the end of a girl's comment about a drawing. I immediately listened.

"Ew, that's the most perverted shit I've ever seen. Is that guy a serial killer?"

"You have to show Everett. Get his ass up out of here."

I stood up and looked at them. She was holding a bar napkin. I stared at the cartoon: Sylvester masturbating his anthropomorphic penis and he crushed Tweety Bird's skull under his foot.

"Who the fuck drew that?" I said.

"Young dude. Red polo. Seemed cool until he gave me this garbage."

"Show that to Everett and get him out of here."

Once the girls were gone, I put on my sweatpants and hoodie and dug the phone number out of the garbage can. I got my shit from my locker and went to the night manager's office to pay my fees.

"What are you in such a hurry for?"

He had never seen me leave this early.

"A friend of mine needs some help."

I could see the far right side of the floor through the one-way mirror. Everett, the bouncer on duty, was already escorting the young man out of his seat.

The night manager looked annoyed and took my fees and I was out the door. I waited in the parking lot to see which car belonged to him. It wasn't Gorgeous George. But the drawing on the napkin was the same. Had I given Vandy the wrong guy? Did I mix up two different men? I couldn't have made a mistake. I saw George drawing those cartoons on the napkins back at the Silver-Dollar. I heard his voice mimic the Looney Toons. I wondered if the dancer made a mistake. Was George still hiding in the corner of the club? I hadn't seen him, and I would have clocked him without even trying. Was it all just a coincidence?

He came out the double doors still putting on his tan jacket. I was going to follow this man in my car, a stupid decision but the fever was back. Everett stood at the entrance, making sure he left. The young man got into a white Toyota pickup and pulled out of the lot. I wasn't far behind. My hands trembled on the steering wheel. I wasn't sure where he was going, another bar, his home, a restaurant. I let two cars merge between us to stay hidden and almost lost him at the next light but caught back up just before the highway ramp. I followed him onto the interstate as he headed south toward the state line. He pulled off onto a sharp exit shrouded in magnolias and dead oaks. We passed a small gas station where I waited a few seconds to put about thirty yards between us. The sun had set and left a heavy murk in place of twilight as storm clouds crowded overhead. It began to sleet. I turned on my windshield wipers. We were the only two cars on the farming road. I took out my phone and called Vandy. I knew I would catch her, she was two hours behind me in the Rocky Mountains.

Her phone rang.

"Hello?"

"Vandy," I said.

"Is this Garland? Garland from North Carolina?"

"Yeah, it's me."

"Thought I recognized your number," she said. "What are you calling about?"

"I'm on a road in the middle of nowhere. A guy came into the club. It wasn't George. But he drew the fuckin' cartoons the same way. I think he's the one, Vandy."

"Are you in trouble?"

"No, Vandy. You don't understand. I was wrong about Gorgeous George. It wasn't him. It's this other guy. He drew a fucked-up picture on a napkin tonight."

"Who is it?"

"Some guy I've never seen before until tonight. He drew the same way."

"Where are you?"

"I'm on the road. I'm behind him. I can give you his plates."

Vandy paused.

"You're following him?" she said.

"Yeah."

"Is it a white pickup truck?"

I swallowed.

"Yes," I said.

"Listen to me, Garland. I know your name isn't Garland, but you need to do exactly as I say. Do you understand?"

"I'm listening."

"Slow your car down and turn around. Then drive as fast as you can. Do not let them get too close behind you."

"What?"

"They're smarter than you. Believe me, they know you're following them. You're being pulled into a trap. Get the fuck out of there!"

"They?"

"Do not drive back home, Garland. If you see the white pickup or a blue jeep, do not go back home. They will find you and they will kill you."

"What the fuck is going on?"

"I don't have the time to explain," she said. "Get off the phone and get out now. Call me when you're safe."

I hung up and slowed the car. I was so scared I grabbed the back of the passenger seat after putting the car in reverse. Navigating through the back windshield, I pressed on the gas and sped down the wrong side of the road. I put about a mile of distance between us before I attempted the three-point turn to get back in the right direction. I sped down the farming road at eighty miles per hour as the monotony of hay bales and tall weeds continued. The sleet came down hard. I was determined not to lose control of my car.

The panic started to fade as I realized the white pickup still hadn't caught up to me. He might not have noticed for a while that I had stopped following him.

I slowed down as I came around the bend and saw the gas station lights in the distance. I was almost out of there.

There was a dip in the road and as soon as I crested the hill, I could see the gas station. That's when a blue jeep pulled out from behind one of the pump stations and parked diagonally on the road.

My hands froze.

I looked at the field to my left. It was just a plain grass field, completely level. I took the chance and drove across the asphalt into the sleet-covered grass. I was gonna drive around the gas station and get on the highway. It could lose them on the highway. I kicked up a trail of half-frozen mud as I sped across the green. The jeep followed.

I kept my foot on the gas pedal. My car undulated like a boat pushing against a choppy current, then my rear bumper sank lower than I had felt before. I had stopped. I floored the gas but nothing happened. Mud splattered across the windshield. I killed the engine. I had to act quick. I was wearing good shoes, my department-store Asics. The gas station was right in front of me. I jumped out of the car and ran across the field into the parking lot and nearly tore open the glass door covered in stickers. The bell rang. I slid across the floor to the elderly man behind the register.

"Please, help me! There's a man after me. He's trying to kill me."

The old man didn't say anything. He blinked and grimaced, then opened up the barrier to the counter. He sat me down on a step stool. I was hidden by the plastic scratch card display, my back to the cigarettes. He took a heavy-looking black revolver from underneath the register and held it in front of him with the barrel pointed at the counter.

I heard a loud pop. The sound was piercing and alien to me. I thought the old man's gun had discharged into the wood of the counter from the way he was holding it. The glass door shattered. The old man dropped to his side in front of me still holding the gun. Blood started to pool around him.

I picked up the revolver. It felt like a brick of solid lead in my hand. The distance between the contoured grip and the trigger was nearly too far for my tiny hand. I had to stretch my index finger to wrap it around that black crescent of cold steel. I imagined the weapon snapping my wrist the second I fired it. I didn't want to fire it, but I had no choice.

The old man started gasping. I wasn't sure what was happening to him, whether he was dying or regaining consciousness. His body spasmed.

I heard the crunch of the glass beyond the counter as the hulking silhouette crossed the threshold into the fluorescent light. I knew I would recognize him if I saw him again. He had a silver pistol in his hand, automatic, the kind cops carried. I don't know anything about guns and I don't ever want to.

I don't remember a lot of what happened after that. The military women at the support group told me that's normal. The stress of the situation keeps you from forming memories or something like that. I never really found out what Gorgeous George and his younger partner were planning for me. Maybe they thought I was another PI or a cop. I only know what everyone else knows about them since the new reports aired: they had a bunker built in the woods on George's property where they kept women in cages. When they were done raping them for days, they lit them on fire and hid their ashes and bone fragments in a giant fire pit. They killed about four girls. I still don't know if Selena was one of them.

Sometime after George entered the gas station but before I walked into the rain and sleet, I took two shots at him and got lucky. The old man's gun was a cannon. The first shot caved in George's thick chest and the second removed the top portion of his skull. White flecks of bone inside thick splatters of ruptured skin and brain tissue drizzled down the bags of pork rings and potato chips. I stood beneath the awning near the locked ice cooler and pebbled garbage can. I wanted to get away from where the dead bodies were. I didn't want to have to look at them or smell them. I wanted to call the police, but I wanted to call Vandy first. I wasn't sure what to do. Looking back, I was in shock. I just stood there holding the gun.

The white pickup sped down the road and swerved into the gas station lot, tires screeching. I shot out his front windshield and the pickup immediately reversed into the main road. I fired every round in the gun until it wouldn't shoot anymore. The sleet hissed on the smoking barrel. I dropped it and the pistol fell to the curb without rebounding. The pickup truck kept reversing into the road until it careened onto its side, halfway hidden in the brambles. It must have fallen into a gulch.

I looked back at Gorgeous George's dead body and tiptoed over the growing puddle of dark blood. I could hear sirens in the distance. A farmer must have heard the gunshots and called the police. I found a phone and dialed 911 anyway.

RETURN OF THE DEATH GOD

Maria listened to a distant woodpecker hammering at the soft pine outside the open window of the motel room just beneath the low, benzedrine-rattle from a next-door AC unit. The air smelled of sour grease and rusted iron. Green pods hanging from a nearby catalpa shook in the muggy nighttime wind.

She noticed a mass of dead Catawba grubs the shape of extinguished cigarettes in the crevice of the plastic-framed sill.

There was no window facing the parking lot, but she had a wide view of its white pebbled gravel through the copper-rimmed aperture in her front door. She caught a brief whiff of pepper by the edge of the doorframe. She lifted the swiveling aluminum cover on the crooked nail to stare out at the discount neon surrounded by leafy darkness, then returned to the opposite side of the box-shaped room; back to the catalpa.

The motel had only one floor but the foundation beyond her view of the flowering tree dropped twelve feet toward a deserted limb of railroad track as if she were looking out from a tower. She stood by the window. There was nothing to sit on but the lonely mattress. The scent of the night air was replaced by a sudden billow of marijuana. Someone was smoking outside, or out a window, hidden in darkness.

She kept a long, blue bottle of *Corralejo* on the nightstand beside the lamp which she poured into a styrofoam cup she had snagged from the lobby. An old woman at the front desk had been taking massive gulps from her stainless steel thermos, getting ready for a long third shift. The display had been set out for the guests and faced the front door. The liquid was dark in the coffee maker and gave off a dismal heat like black sunlight. She took the cup and the woman didn't notice. The look of the bubbling coffee left her with a deep hunger, which she could only satisfy with what she had brought with her; it was too much trouble to find the nearest store in this foreign town. She had a few tortillas in aluminum foil and some buffalo jerky wrapped in parchment paper.

She opened the nightstand drawer out of half-drunken curiosity and saw only an English language bible and the yellowing pages of a South Carolina/Georgia roadmap.

Maria saw the bean pods hanging from the lone tree and felt the ruff texture of loose fibers tightening around her throat. She coughed. The image of young men swinging from the further pines haunted her view; young black men floating in starched suits, some with rope and others with barbed wire set alight like hanging torches. All this time the *gringos* had been crossing over to get drunk, screw girls, and start fights in her bordertown and, yet, they had done worse to their own people. The scent wafting into her room had gone from the herbal, sweet stench of marijuana to the antique musk of tobacco. Whoever had been smoking in the dark was trying to throw off the scent. Still able to see the memories of lynched men's agonized expressions, she closed the window.

She sat alone and swallowed another sip of tequila (she preferred whiskey, but the *Corralejo* was all she had with her) and ate another tortilla.

Someone knocked at the door three times.

She made no sound as she peered through the hole in the door: a younger white man in a green camouflage shirt with a breast pocket and a worn baseball cap. He had a five o'clock shadow. This boy was most likely the foreman's son she had been told about with the under-the-table work.

She spoke reluctantly.

"Who is it?"

"Soy yo, hijo de el charro."

El Charro? What kind of 19th-century indentured servant had taught this kid Spanish? She could forgive the bad grammar, but why use such a word?

"Who?"

"I got the...trabajo. You're looking for trabajo, right?"

"What's your name?"

"Billy."

They had told her his name would be Billy.

"Okay, Billy. I'm going to open the door."

She took the pruner knife from her bag and tucked it into her back pocket, then retracted the deadbolt and removed the chain.

He stepped inside and sat down on the bed, leaving her standing over him awkwardly to close the door.

"Sorry, I've been on my feet all day long."

He rubbed his knees through his pants.

"You speak English?"

"A little," she said.

"Yeah, I been tryin' to pick what Spanish I can from whoever I can pick it up from. But that ain't the way to do it. Least not for me. I don't have the time though to take a class and I wouldn't know where to find one to sign up for. Am I talking too fast?"

"What?"

"You understand me? Me intender?"

She wanted to correct his grammar but it seemed improper since he was offering her work.

He reached into his pocket and she became tense. Her hand grazed the outline of the collapsed pruner blade behind her.

He took out the contents of his jeans: his car keys, a pack of cigarettes, a lighter, and a folded scrap of computer paper. He left everything strewn out on the bed and unfolded the corners of the white paper.

"This is...uh...directions to the farm. You'll need'em." He handed her the rigid sheet. "You don't got a car do you?" he said.

"I'm going to ride with Luella."

"Okay. Well, I brought you that just in case. People's rides fall through all the time. Folks end up walking. If you have to walk you can follow those directions just as well, but you need to get goin' about an hour early. It's an hour on foot, right? Don't be late. Being late get's the old man ticked off more than anything. I know time is funny to you people, but in America time is money."

She glanced at the directions.

"I understand."

"How long you been in the States?"

"A while," she said.

"I figured. You speak good English."

"Thank you."

"How long you been in SC?"

"Essee?"

"South Carolina."

"Four days."

"So you need some work then?"

"I could always use work."

"I heard that. Way it works with us is, we take you on for the day, sunup to sundown, and then we pay cash for the day. When you get your cash, we'll tell you if we wanna see you tomorrow. If you get to come back the next day, you can bet we'll need you the rest of the week. Now, it isn't a honeymoon. Just cause you work for us for a while don't mean we'll need you forever. Everyday you work for us, you got to see it as temporary. Now, tomorrow when you work, I can pretty much guarantee that you'll get your cash and the word, the word as to whether we'll need you to come back. There's gonna be days when you'll get the word, but we can't get you your cash. You'll have to respect that and wait a day for your money. Banks take holidays and other shit. Just the way it is. Understand?"

"I understand," she said.

"Good, that's good. And another thing, you don't know us. You don't know us and we don't know you. Anybody asks, anybody in plain clothes or a suit, you just shrug and say you don't speak any fuckin' English. Say one thing about us and we call ICE and you go back where you came from."

"I understand."

"Then we understand each other," he said, scooping up his pack and lighter from the bed linen. "I'm gonna open your window here."

She watched him as he stepped to the other end of the room and opened her window. He lit a cigarette and blew the smoke, uselessly, into the center of the room. He pointed with his glowing ember at the tracks below.

"Hasn't been a train through this town since I was ten years old. Used to stay up at night and listen to the whistle blaring. You could hear it and see the lights across the fields like it was going somewhere better than here."

She watched him as he stared at the tracks.

He asked her if she missed Mexico.

"No," she said. "But I miss my son."

"He back home? With the husband? Grandfolks?"

"No."

Billy didn't say anything. He pointed to the bottle of tequila.

"That'll have to be our little secret."

She went silent as he walked over to the nightstand and picked up the bottle to read the label.

"You mind?"

She handed him her cup.

He plucked the cork from the top.

"Nah, I'm not prudish," he said before drinking it straight. He wiped his bristled chin. "That's better than anything I've had lately."

She placed the cup on the TV set.

He put the bottle down on the nightstand and barely attempted to put the cork in the top. He turned to her and stroked her chin as he took a deep drag from the cigarette.

"You're a little older but you're still pretty," he said. "Any white man ever tell you you're pretty?"

"A few," she said, letting him touch her.

He moved his hand to her shoulder.

"You know there's things you can do to guarantee you a job."

"What kinds of things?"

"Fun things mostly. Fun things we could do right here."

"Yeah?"

"Yeah."

She moved his hand off her shoulder.

"What if I don't want to do that? What if I just want to work?"

He shrugged.

"How bad do you want to work though? You know? Everybody wants to come through and work. How are you gonna stand out? I'm a good lover, I'm sure you'll end up liking it anyway. Don't nobody have to know. Let me kiss you."

"What?"

"Just let me kiss you."

He stood over her, looking down. His prick was hard, he rubbed it against her belly button.

She could see him taking women away in his truck, bending them over behind hay bales, young girls and old women, pulling at their hair like rope.

"I don't want you to kiss me," she said. "I don't know you. Maybe we go do something later after I work for you."

He forced her hand onto his crotch.

"Come on, you gonna pass this up? Feel it. That's some serious equipment. You can't tell me no Mexican ever had one like that." He placed his thumb over her lips. "You want to work or not?"

"Put that out. I don't like the smell."

She gestured toward the cigarette in his hand.

"Oh, sorry," he said and flicked the cigarette out the window.

He grabbed the bottle and took a mouthful, swished loudly, and spit the liquor out the window in a visible mist like a shaman blessing a sacred space.

"That should take care of the breath," he said.

"Why do you want to kiss me?"

"I wanna do more than just kiss you."

She went toward her bag and got out a small travel bottle of shampoo.

"I want you to be clean. You've worked all day."

He grabbed the back of her hair and pushed her against the wall. She faced him. He took both her wrists and squeezed them together with the power of his single hand. The shampoo dropped to the floor.

"You don't exactly smell like a desert rose yourself. You wanna work in this country, tax-free, leaching off the rest of us, you gonna have to put out once in a while. Nobody rides free."

He tightened his grip on her hair and shoved her across the room, deliberately tripping her on his boot. She missed the bed and burned her forearms across the carpet. He noticed the pruner knife in her back pocket.

"Don't fucking move," he said as he took the blade. "The hell kind of piece-of-shit tool is this?"

"It's for branches and sticks."

He tapped the blade against his knee.

"Ain't too sharp. What, were you going to stab me with this if I got too rough?"

Her face was hidden in her hair. She remained on the floor.

"It was sharp enough for you," she said.

"The fuck you talking about?" he said, cleaning the dirt from under his thumb with the hooked edge.

"It was sharp enough for you to use on her," she said in a much more fluid, American-English voice. "When you started to cut her. It was sharp enough then. You carved designs in her back. You slashed open one of her breasts. You tore into her face. Then you raped her. You stuffed her face into the pillow and suffocated her so no one could hear her screaming. She died and you were still raping her."

"I haven't done anything like that to anybody."

"Not yet. But you do eventually. Next few minutes in fact. You do it every night. Over and over again."

He collapsed the blade and tossed it aside, then put his things back in his pockets.

"What are you like an undercover cop or something?"

"How could a cop know what you're about to do before you do it?"

"You're fuckin' with my mind. Are you trying to pin something on me?"

"I'm just telling you what you did."

"I'm out of here. You're a fuckin' psycho. You can forget about work."

"You knew in the back of your mind when you saw her, she wasn't gonna make it to work the next day."

He went for the door and tried to open it. The bolt was loose and the chain had been unhooked, but the door wouldn't budge.

"Let me out!"

"I can't let you out."

"Let me out of your room."

"This is your room now."

He set both his feet on the wall and pulled at the door-knob, prying it off the door as he fell onto the bed. He lay there, holding the broken knob.

"What is this?"

She was still facedown on the floor. Her voice carried through the room, echoing within his thoughts.

"This is your corner of the Mictlān."

A brown hawk carrying a limp rattlesnake in its claw flew inside through the window. The massive raptor draped the snake carcass along the television set and perched itself beside it, clicking its claws on the worn plastic, knocking away the styrofoam cup

Maria's image rose from the floor, still horizontal, float-ing above him, her hair fluttering as if suspended in water. A golden aura shimmered along the silhouette of her face, which appeared to him as an exposed skull. She reached out her hand and the hawk flew to her wrist.

"Who are you?"

She said nothing and passed through the ceiling.

He stared down at his hands and only saw blood. There was blood on the sheets, blood on his abdomen, blood smeared on the headboard of the bed where Maria lay, her face in the pillow. He had blood underneath his fingernails.

A GOOD JOB

I had nicknames for most of them (Ex-Meth, Lizard Man, The Beach Nazi) except for Sylvia who was in mid-transition, and Buck who was half-Cherokee. The other guys called Sylvia the Trap, and Buck the Half-Breed. Retail grocery could be ugly behind the facade of bright lights and clean shelves.

Winter Haven's Super Markets Inc. was expanding up the East Coast and a lot of ex-warehouse and CDL driver types were looking to get a piece of the employee-owned stock that came after a two-year commitment. Very few made it that long. Even guys with years of experience in the stocking game, like myself, couldn't keep up with the workload at Winter Haven's. The job was especially rough on your legs. Shin splints and brittle knees were the most common outcome of a life lived between the aisles.

I had worked at a health-food store for three years and thought I knew what I was doing when I joined the major chain. My first sixteen-hour shift changed my mind.

The worst part of the gig was the third shift just before inventory day. We had a baby-faced twenty-year-old assistant manager who liked to keep us well past sunrise after an entire night of running prep. Jason, the born-again former meth junkie from Pensacola, was exhausted, drifting in and out of sleep behind the wheel of a forklift with a four-hundred-pound stack of commercial firewood teetering on the edge of a twelve-foot-high pallet. When he was well-rested, Jason was unstoppable. High on the newfound drug of the Holy Spirit, he'd practically attack a truckload of heavy-volume stock when the rest of us were spent. They told me he had been a house painter when he was still mainlining crank in the devil's armpit that was the Gulf of Mexico. I imagined him painting an entire block of oceanfront condos in one fevered afternoon. Jason had an obese, invalid wife who blamed him for their son's death. Buck told me she was hideous and mean and relied on Jason for basic things like showers and going to the bathroom. Jason was my direct superior and he liked me because I listened to his biblical theories and never teased him about his wife, which usually meant he chose me to stick by his side for overtime while he avoided home.

The best part of the gig was getting picked for nightly resets. A reset meant we were rearranging the layout of the store. They'd shut it down early, truck in fresh shelving and, again, we'd work through the night. Usually, we'd make it out by one or two in the morning. We didn't have to wear uniforms or deal with customers. Sometimes music was allowed. But it was the comradery that made it what it was. Everyone was tethered to the same chain, digging the same ditch. You didn't get that from the regular store experience, regular hours. It was all about moving up. Up, up and out. Get your money and kick down the ladder.

I left the health food shop because of the pay, but there had been other perks like all the cheap drugs for sale at the deli kitchen. Everyone there seemed to do other things besides work. We had musicians and artists and girls who could read auras. The assistant manager used to follow the Dead and my grocery supervisor was an amateur gecko breeder. For the reasonable paycheck at Haven's, I had to shave off my beard and tuck in my shirt, and take the verbal abuse of a former marine who smoked menthol cigarettes and drank diet mountain dew all day. I had never worked for a company that insisted upon its quasi-dogma before. Every store had a little shrine in the corner with the founder's glowing image as if he were some kind of deity. Jason had come to believe that there was something vaguely godlike about the founder, that the mission of Winter Haven's was the continuation of the loaves and fishes miracle from the Gospel of Matthew.

I had a 4 am to 1 pm shift. I was driving to work early in the dark. I used to think of myself as a top-notch laborer, but now I was a problem guy, a wise ass. I couldn't keep my back-stock floats neat enough and I was getting written up each day I couldn't get the surplus out. It had been three days so far. I was never able to touch the surplus since the truck shipments took me my whole shift. The brief mornings we might have gotten a chance to run some surplus, we could only afford to spare an hour at the most. By the end of the day, when we hit the replenishment cycle with the scanner guns we were fucked to know how to cut off all the doubled-up excess tags pushing the useless stock. You had ten minutes to the end of your shift. You just held your breath and patched the holes in the shelves and tripled up on the staples you knew would sell out over a day. I was headed south on the highway toward the store when I stopped, pulling the car over to the shoulder on the Catawba River Bridge. I could see the lights in the distance, lights from a North Carolina township glimmering along the black surface of the river which crossed the state line. It was three-thirty in the morning. There were no other cars on the road. I hoisted myself up onto the ledge. I couldn't see in the dark, but I knew from where I stood there were some boulders below.

I quit my job the next day. I said to myself that no company or individual would ever put me on a ledge again. I'd rather be a murderer than end up on that ledge in the dark. Buck called me after I hung up my apron.

"What the hell, man? If you were unhappy, you could have just transferred departments."

"If I left grocery, there'd be nobody in that department."

"There's nobody left now, asshole."

"It had to be a clean break, man. I couldn't look those guys in the face every day from another department."

"You idiot. Winter Haven's stock is going through the roof. You could have been a millionaire by the time you hit thirty."

"Yeah, that's the dream they sell ya."

"You son of a bitch."

"Goodbye, Buck."

The first thing I did was contact my old boss at the health-food store. I didn't want to seem too desperate. We were still on good terms and often spoke after I left. I worked like a madman in my last two weeks and hoped they'd rehire me. I texted him but he never responded.

Four days later, I began to feel a little more desperate. My last check from Winter Haven's had come through and I had some money saved up. I'd be screwed after paying rent and electricity next month. I went into Greenpoint Grocery and headed to the deli counter under the guise of buying some pot. I found Damion on the grill and started bullshiting. I bought a gram and had him make me a turkey sandwich. I finally asked about Lizard Man.

"Oh, yeah. Kyle don't work here no more."

"What happened?"

"He had a fuckin' meltdown with the new manager and just quit on the spot."

"God fuckin' dammit."

Not long after that fruitless visit, Kyle the Lizard Man texted me back asking if they were hiring any good men at Winter Haven's. I told him we were both up shit creek.

"I probably couldn't pass the drug test anyway," he said.

Over the next few months, I abstained from doing any coke or smoking weed. I applied for a few more grocery gigs and a liquor store job. Both jobs required cash-register skills. I was a fucking klutz with money. I couldn't balance a till to save my life. I was a backroom guy, a laborer. I couldn't imagine going into something like food service. My car was too beat up to qualify for a ridesharing app.

Another couple of weeks went by. I applied for some warehouse jobs. I had canceled my internet connection after paying rent. I had to check my email at the library or use the McDonald's wifi on the phone which I also couldn't afford for much longer.

Kyle gave me a call to ask if I had any coke to sell him. His regular guy was in jail. I had a half-baggie I wasn't planning on snorting till I had work. We agreed to meet at his house. He answered the door in his pajamas and a white undershirt. He had a gecko on his wrist.

"What's up, man?"

"Not much."

"You got a job yet?"

"No," I said.

"Well, maybe I can help you with that."

There was a little girl in the living room watching *Sesame Street*.

"I'm watching my niece today," he said, as he set the gecko inside the terrarium. He turned to the girl. "Hey, sweetie? Uncle Kyle's gonna talk to his friend real quick, then I'm gonna make us lunch ok?"

She nodded in silence.

We passed through the hall and up the carpeted stairs to his bedroom.

"You can smoke in here as long as we're upstairs. My sister just doesn't like it if we smoke around Kiley," he said as he lit a Newport Menthol.

"Kiley?"

"Yeah, she named her after me."

"What does your sis do?"

"You don't remember? She's a sales rep at Kay Jewelers."

I stared back down the steps and lit a Camel.

"You sure about leaving her alone in front of the TV?"

"She's not going anywhere. She's a good kid, easy to deal with. One of my geckos bit her the other day and she took it like a champ. Plus I'm not trying to buy yayo in front of her."

He handed me the money and I gave him the half-gram. He set it in his bedside drawer.

"So, what have you got that might help me. Cause I'll be honest with you, I'm fuckin' broke. I was gonna use this money to get lunch and dinner."

"You're that strapped? Damn, dude. Tell you what, why don't you stick around for hot dogs and a couple of brews and wait till my brother-in-law get's back."

"That'd be nice. What's he got?"

"He's got some under-the-table work. I can vouch for you."

"What if he says no?"

Kyle shrugged.

"Then no hard feelings?"

"Alright."

We ate hotdogs in the living room and watched *Dora the Explorer* with his niece and drank a couple of cans of Busch until his brother-in-law showed up. He was a short guy but extremely muscular. His hair was moussed and he carried a heavy gym bag around his shoulder. He was dark; either Italian or Hispanic. I didn't ask. He took off his Raybans in the living room and pointed at me with them.

"This one of your butt buddies, Kyle?" he said in front of his daughter.

"No, this is Joey. He's from my old team at Greenpoint."

"Yeah?"

"He doesn't have a job either right now. Just left Winter Haven's."

"That company's coming up. Sounds like a poor decision to leave."

"Well, Eddy. That's kind of what I wanted to talk to you about," Kyle said standing up. "Let's go to the garage alone for a second."

Eddy looked at me then followed Kyle into the hall.

I waited a few minutes, watching *Dora* with the little girl. I knew I wasn't gonna get it, whatever house-painting or moving gig he had on the side. I could tell this guy didn't like me, didn't like coming home to see a stranger in his house next to his daughter, draining beers in front of the TV. I'd tell Kyle it was no hard feelings, get the hell out of there and buy some more alcohol to feel sorry for myself at home.

Kyle's voice echoed down the hall.

"Joey, come on in."

I stood up and left the girl in the living room and headed for the garage door in the hall. I walked in and Eddy pointed a gun to my face. I was steady. I stared down the barrel. I could tell it was a .9mm knockoff Italian. Kyle was smoking a cigarette behind him.

"I told you. He doesn't flinch," he said.

"No, he doesn't," Eddy said, hesitating before he lowered the gun. "You ever killed anybody?"

"Nope," I said.

"You ever try?"

I shook my head.

"Anybody ever try to kill you?"

"Yup."

"Okay," he said, nodding his head. "I don't need a career criminal. I need somebody who knows when to lay low and when to walk away. But I can't have someone afraid of bringing the heavy neither."

"Those two traits are rare in somebody willing to do something illegal."

"I know. And Kyle says you got'em."

I paused for a moment.

"So, are you gonna let me into the fold or what?"

"We pull this off, I never want to see you again. I get a bad feeling and pull the plug, I never want to see you again. It's a safety thing. We don't know each other anymore. Now, you two have a connection. That worries me. I'm gonna need you to tourniquet that shit from this point on. We got to think about business. The reason people go to jail is because they don't plan not to. Are we in agreement?"

"I agree," I said.

He turned to Kyle.

"Are we in agreement?"

"I got'chu."

"Alright," Eddy said, clapping his hands together. "Let's talk details."

I didn't sleep the night before. I lied in bed and thought about the job. It was a smash and grab. A thirty-year-old parolee in the East Washington apartments, Unit 7G, was selling molly, Xanax, codeine, and massive amounts of weed. He was small-time, but word had gotten around that he had about fifteen grand in cash in a safe. Eddy told us he had a friend the dealer couldn't link back to us case the place for him during some controlled buys. He was on parole, that's why he didn't deal in the harder stuff. Eddy figured he wouldn't have a gun on him either. I called bullshit on that assumption.

"If he's selling and he's already got a safe, he'll have a gun. Maybe not an AR-15, but the motherfucker'll carry a pistol on him."

The name of the game was in and out. We had to subdue this guy the minute we kicked in the door, then grab the cash and run. He lived alone according to Eddy.

I took a shower in the morning and put on some drab clothing. I forced myself to eat an egg with toast. I didn't want to eat but I knew I would get sick if I didn't. I got in my car and sipped a Monster as I drove to Kyle and Eddy's place. There was a heavy thunderstorm on its way. The edge of the horizon was nearly black with dark clouds while the sky overhead was still bright. The green energy drink was sweet and my heart raced as I sipped. I had my loaded .357 in the glove box. When I got to Kyle's place, I took it out and shoved it in my belt loop. I sat on the hood of my car and drank my Monster. A minute later, the garage door opened and piled into Eddy's Honda. Each moment felt empty and painfully quiet. Kyle looked back at me from the shotgun seat.

"Think of it like going to work," he said. "Just let your instincts take over."

"You have breakfast?" Eddy said.

"Yeah."

"Poor decision. I never eat before a job."

"You worried I'm gonna throw up?"

"No, it's just good to stay hungry. Keep your thoughts lean."

"How many times have you done this?"

"A few," Eddy said.

I looked at Kyle.

"You?"

"Once," he said.

It was raining when we got there. The gutter was swelling with dirty water. The guy's unit was one flight up the concrete and metal stairwell. I didn't like it. It was too easy to see us coming. A guy could shoot back at us as we escaped.

"There's no other exit?"

"One way in, one way out."

"Don't park the car here. It's too close."

"Are you in charge now?"

"You can't let him know what your car looks like if he catches a glimpse through the window. Park over by those mailboxes."

Eddy didn't acknowledge me but followed my direction just the same. We got out of the car and my stomach dropped. I checked my belt to make sure I had my gun underneath my shirt. We headed through the rain and up the stairwell. Our footfalls echoed through the open-air corridor as we approached the dealer's front door.

Eddy knocked with the butt of his pistol. We saw the light in the peephole dim. Someone was looking through. I hung back with Kyle at the edge of the railing.

"What can I do for you, friend?"

Eddy kept his gun out of sight and flashed a twenty-dollar bill at the peephole.

"Looking to get a gram?"

"I don't know you, man."

"Come on, man. I'm from out of town. I just wanted to buy some quality bud and smoke it alone in my hotel room. I have back problems."

I shook my head. He was talking too much. That's not how a smash and grab is supposed to work. I took a deep breath and pushed Eddy out of the way as I drew my pistol. I shot out the lock and kicked the door open. The young guy was pushed back by the force of the door. I bashed him upside the head with the hot barrel of the .357 and turned him onto his stomach. I sat on his hand with my knees and pressed the gun against his face.

"Where's the safe?"

"I ain't got no safe."

I started beating in his face with the butt of the gun.

Kyle and Eddy were shuffling through the apartment like idiots. One of them tried to close the door even though I had shot out the knob. The hole was big enough to stick your hand through. The chain hadn't been set which made it easier to kick open.

"Where the fuck is your safe, motherfucker?"

"It's in the closet by the bedroom."

Eddy and Kyle moved into the bedroom and opened up the closet.

"What's the code?"

"6675."

I looked up at Eddy.

"You got that?"

I heard the beeps as he pressed the buttons on the keypad.

"It ain't openin'," he said.

I pressed the barrel of the gun against the dealer's head.

"I'm gonna fuckin' kill you."

"You got to hit pound first! You got to hit pound, for fuck's sake."

"It's a safe, not a cellphone. You think we're fuckin' stupid?"

"It's a custom keypad. I swear to God."

I heard Eddy frantically punching in the code.

The safe opened and Kyle grabbed the money and threw it into his black backpack. Small rolls of wrinkled bills mostly and a few crisp stacks of twenties.

"Let's go," I said.

Eddy and Kyle were still going through the safe, stealing bottles of pills and bags of weed.

"Let's go," I said. "We're gone. It's over."

I looked up from the living room. Kyle and Eddy were still raiding the safe. There was a figure behind them. My adrenaline surged. The girl standing there was so still, I thought she was a poster for a split second, then realized she had been hiding in the bathroom. She had a Glock in her raised hand and fired it. The muzzle flash and smoke looked so foreign in the small bedroom. Kyle went down with the bag in his hand. The side of his head was blackened with spurting blood. I jumped off the dealer's body and ran out the door. Eddy was close behind me, but the parolee pushed himself off the carpet and tackled him into the kitchen. The girl fired another shot and I felt the force of the bullet crush my shoulder blade. I fell down the concrete steps. My pistol slipped from my hands and discharged as it landed. I dragged myself into a corner. I was bleeding down my side. I could hear sirens in the distance. I heard more yelling from the unit above and then four gunshots. Eddy was probably dead. I reached over with my good hand and grabbed my pistol since it was registered in my name, then dragged myself down the corridor where the apartments ended. The lightning flashed overhead. I threw myself into the elephant grass and reeds beside the creek.

I stared upward at the falling rain, hidden in the coarse stands of green, and fell asleep.

JAYBIRD

People said there was at least ten years' worth of rage and humiliation in the ten minutes it took Jaybird to beat the Foreman to death. Longest ten minutes on earth. He never let up. His hands looked like they'd been through a meat grinder by the time he was done. Halfway through, the Foreman stopped asking for help and just looked stunned at how badly he was getting hit. It must have been the kind of pain that stops you dead in your tracks and keeps you from thinking, the kind of pain where you don't even have the strength to cuss. Later, we realized he'd been trying to take in a breath but couldn't.

The Foreman had been over everyone on a big site a year and a half back closer to the low country and a lot of guys at the Cazador, no different than Jaybird, had put in time on that project. It was a big deal when the bottom dropped out. The state government got involved. Jobs and the money along with them had vanished. People got no notice. The paychecks just never came. But that wasn't what Jaybird was trying to settle with his fists that night. Far as we understood, the Foreman probably got screwed like everyone else.

We still don't know why the Foreman, or the ex-Foreman we should say, came to the Cazador the night Jeremiah went to jail, but, after seeing something like that, it didn't matter. We say he came 'to' the Cazador and not 'into' the Cazador because he never made it inside. Jeremiah clocked him between the parking lot and the front door and ran out after him. People didn't start referring to him as Jeremiah until he'd been sent upstate, before that we just called him Jaybird. We all drank on the weekends at this old Mexican restaurant. It was just a dive saloon in reality, but the county law prohibited selling drinks without serving food and, over time, the poorly conceived family restaurant turned into one of the roughest spots along the highway.

Jaybird decked him like a linebacker. The Foreman was an older man, closer to his sixties, and he looked to be in pretty good shape. Jaybird wasn't even thirty yet. He didn't say anything. Didn't give a warning, and he certainly didn't give the old guy any quarter to try to defend himself; show him how tough an old-timer could be. We'd seen plenty of scraps that went the other way on the younger guys, but Jaybird just went for him like he wasn't gonna get the chance ever again. He had him on the dirt, his knees pinning down his hands when he first socked him with a left hook. He seemed to let gravity do the work as he brought down his balled fist right into the center of the old man's face. He was only using his left at first. The old man's angered voice carried through to the bar. It wasn't until Jaybird started using both fists with a vicious rhythm that the man began weeping and calling for help. Instead, we all circled around the spectacle, beers in hand, transfixed. It's a dangerous place to hit someone, the face. The bones are small and sharp and cause injury, especially with bare fists. As the beating continued, we could see Jaybird's knuckles turn from pink like a rash to raw-meat red once their blood started to mingle. The Foreman's nose hadn't flattened completely yet, but it had definitely split. Bits of the skin over Jay's knuckles and fingers peeled away as he kept wailing on the old man. Odd thing about fights in the real world, they're pretty much silent. Unless the two parties are yelling, fists make little sound. We could all hear the muted slaps of Jay's knuckles crashing into the tanned leather hide of the old timer's skin. Jaybird leaned in and pressed the man's head down against the earth and started taking long, heavy blows that used the whole right side of his body against his ear. Darkness pooled up beneath the old man's skin. We heard things snapping and cracking like ice being crushed in a plastic bag. The contours of his face changed and, finally, the old man was left alone on the ground twitching as if he were having a seizure. He didn't get back up. His eyes flickered around like he had'em fixed on some insect. He wasn't talking. He was just making dribbled noises with his mouth.

Jaybird stood up with his mangled hands and, through his labored exertions, mumbled something about telling his mom he was sorry. He went inside to run his hands under cold water in the restroom while we stayed out and watched the Foreman twitch and babble.

Darnell's girl said that Jaybird turned the guy retarded. That's when we heard Jaybird's voice behind say, "No, I didn't. I killed him."

People were offering to give Jaybird a gun to finish it, but he didn't want it. The law came right after that and cuffed him and took him away. The ambulance also pulled in, but it was done.

By doing nothing, we had all participated in a murder. Jaybird didn't tell on anybody. There was a lot of paranoia around town, thinking he'd make a move for a reduced sentence, but the law never came for us.

Things didn't move on from that night. I think that's because we never figured out what the man had done to Jeremiah. No one wanted to look into it because they were afraid of getting found out as one of the people who stood and watched him do it. But we needed to know. I think a lot about it. And I think that's why we stood and watched. We might have thought, in some unconscious part of our minds, that the answers would come out of the beating somehow and we'd see why our friend, in a split second in time, threw away his life. But all we got was an ending to the story.

Francisco called me around four in the morning, which was fine 'cause I was coming off of the Friday night of a three-day weekend still drunk and slouched in a booth at the after-hours spot on the hill. The Crazy Horse strip joint on Cherry had closed for good, along with the Money and Scandals and the whorehouse on Celanese. There wasn't much left to do on a Saturday morning except go home with some Pedialyte and a bag of weed and try and stave off the hangover. Cherry Road was a bad place anyway with the college being so close and all that jailbait and violent frathouse kids living near. Best to go north and keep drinking at Morgan's where people your own age crashed out at the end of the line. The phone was buzzing along the table knocking over warm, sticky brown-glass bottles. I answered the phone and told him where I was. He said he was coming down the road and wanted to go to the Catawba Reservation and pick up some dope. So he picked me up and we drove out to the sticks and knocked on the Boyler brothers' door and scored some red phosphorus crank and took it out to the lake to slam it. We were practicing karate in the dark. whacked out of our minds, when Francisco mentioned Jeremiah again. I hadn't known Francisco back in those days. I didn't know he'd been in South Carolina that long. The Texan started going on about how he worked with Jaybird on the Santee Cooper nuclear project years ago.

"You knew the Foreman whose ass he beat?"

"Yeah, he was over all of us, day guys."

"What was he like?"

"He was a son of a bitch."

"Bad to Jaybird?"

"Oh, yeah. Real bad. I'd call him a sadist to tell you the truth."

"Like what'd he do to him?"

"Just like stuff. You know how it is."

The sun came up and we were still wired playing video games in Francisco's living room. We'd been talking so long we'd forgotten what we were talking about, and we had both sweat through our jeans and t-shirts. Around noon, I told him I had to get back home and we shook hands. I crossed the railroad tracks and walked off into the daylight. On the way, I passed the Cazador. It had shut down maybe a couple of months after the beating. The parking lot had been taken over by wrinkled patterns of crabgrass and tall purple blooms of bull thistle. The tropical plants left by the last owners had all turned the same shade of brown as the fake-adobe stucco. Wasps had fused their nests with the corners of the outdoor walls just beneath the gutter. The interior was covered in dirt, scraps of paper, and stale leaves. An antiquated dishwasher unit had been hauled outside close to the gnarly wisteria vine, and below the kudzu-shrouded gulch lay a pit with hundreds of spent bottles. I kicked up a few wild sweet-potato vines and sat on a patch of chickweed. The bald patch of dirt where the Foreman once lay was about three feet from my boots. I sat and stared for a long time.

It was close to a year after the Boyler brothers' place was raided by federal agents that we started hearing rumors about Jeremiah getting out. Francisco's son claimed he saw him at the Save-a-Lot buyin' up eggs and cans of beans. Tommy and the boys said they knew Jeremiah was going up and down I-85 looking for work. Somebody said he was in a halfway house in Columbia. A couple of the guys who ran the machine shop said they found him standing out by the York County Lowe's looking for under-the-table work with the Honduran expats. It didn't seem like he'd been in prison all that long.

I was sitting with a cleaner cut group back on the hill inside the after-hours joint in December. Two other guys in that group, excluding Francisco, had seen the beating first hand.

That's when Jaybird, looking a hell of a lot older than his days by now, walked into the bar with knee pads and tattered jeans covered in chalky flecks of drywall. His coat looked donated and his hat was a shade darker on the crown of his head from excess sweat. His hands were withered and callused and bony. We watched him in silence as he took a seat at the booth and ordered a Dr. Pepper and Vodka. No one said anything to him. He sat and drank and looked at a cellphone with his enormous hand and paid for each drink as they came.

Nobody acknowledged him, but silence had settled over the bar.

He took a piss in the men's stall and walked outside for a cigarette.

A few of us decided to go outside for a smoke as well.

Everyone was standing outside in the cold, half-sobered up, watching Jaybird. I locked eyes with him and, instead of looking away, gave him a nod.

"Hey, you Jaybird?"

"Who's asking?"

I let him know I was Teddy's cousin from Clover.

He gave a subtle nod of recognition.

"Okay," he said. "Yeah, we worked on the Hampton Inn by the airport with Teddy and Russell."

"Yeah," I said, holding out my hand. "Welcome home."

He shook it and we bullshitted for another few minutes then it got late and he said he had to be at work in the morning and got inside a beat-up looking truck and drove off down the street. Before he left though, he rolled the window down and called my name. I said, "Yeah?" He said thanks. Nobody's seen him since.

A KIND OF HUNTER

She sat in a chain coffee shop separated from the rest of the Tampa airport by four walls of clear glass, flanked by two Floridians who, in her mind, had become ambassadors to the state. There was a small woman in a grey pantsuit typing on a laptop as she spoke into a headset about summaries of information and what she would do to spearhead certain tasks next time she spoke to Craig, whoever Craig was. At her other shoulder, a man, also typing on a laptop, kept cursing under his breath.

"Fuck. Jesus, fuck."

He stared into a screen crowded with shifting statistics.

She sipped her coffee and relished the air-conditioning. She wondered what kind of frozen netherworld one had to come from to find Florida the least bit charming, and how no one else on the sidewalks besides her would sweat. Steam rose in ghostly mists from the sunbaked roads after every rainstorm.

No, Kari could never call Florida home, but that's where one had to go to find people like exiled Cuban poets and troublesome marine biologists who may or may not have known about a certain energy firm's interest in the mangrove forests. She saw to it that bad luck would strike twice, that exiled poets tended to drink themselves into a coma before falling off the boardwalk, that activist biologists could go missing while out in their pontoon boats. These were things she could only do in Florida. Now she could go home with her Everglades tan and a new pair of expensive sunglasses.

She finished her morning coffee while doing her best not to rub shoulders with the loud strangers in the adjacent seats, then went to a magazine stand. There, she read an entire article in an upscale magazine with an ink and pastel cartoon on its cover. She was so entranced by the article about a strange new sub-economy people of her generation had spawned that, by the time the writer's spell was broken, Kari only had five minutes to board her flight. She remembered her alias being called over the PA system at Logan once when she figured she still had ten minutes to spare. Not here, boarding was tedious in the South, even in Florida, a strangely unsouthern Dixie state. She got on the plane and waited another eight minutes as a gathering of loose, floral shirts and street-vendor-bought Panama hats filled out the seats.

They took off and she thought about the snows of Montana to cool herself, about her father with his German name and South American accent: a Chilean survivalist. He was the reason she could speak Spanish. She thought about him storing rotten cantaloupes for the winter snows, spray painting them black, and sticking them on two-by-fours in the field. He would drive her around on the snowmobile as she practiced her aim with a beretta or the family Winchester.

Her mother, the woman from whom she had inherited her first name, was not Chilean. She was Finnish. Unlike Spanish, Kari never spoke Finnish in the house and her mother had no interest in teaching her. Her father made the decisions for their small household and life on the range was seldom placid. She recalled a beating she had received in the kitchen and stopped thinking about Montana altogether.

She thought about killing the poet, meeting him at the little grass-hut bar on the dunes as the rainstorm closed in, blowing the palmettos and banana leaves and the loose collar of his *playero* sideways. He wasn't a lecher and she didn't need to use her looks to disarm him. Getting close was easy because he was lonely, respectful, and lonely like a grandfather. Something she said had tipped him off that she was part-Chilean. She thought she had said "*a pata*" rather than the usual "*a pie*," or perhaps she had snuck a "*me tinca*" into the mix of her speech.

The plane touched down in the midafternoon. She pulled her luggage along the gray carpet of the terminal, then took the escalator to the parking garage. She unlocked the black Nissan sedan and crouched low to check the underside of her car with a tactical flashlight. A manila envelope had been taped to the bottom. She checked the insides of the tires for loose wires or anything foreign and cylindrical. She stepped inside after placing her luggage in the passenger seat, counted the money (she was a grand short) in the envelope, and drove out of the garage. After paying the man in the tollbooth, she turned onto the city street and headed to its center. She bought an empanada from the food truck in the park and ate it with one hand as she drove home. The Nissan left the city and took briefly to the highway. She noticed a similar vehicle from outside the airport then retreated into the countryside. She passed a few small farms, flowers and soy mostly, nothing big enough for cows. One pasture had a pony and another housed a few goats and barn dogs, the little terriers used for purging rats. She slowed the car as she pulled into a wooded cul-de-sac and parked on the gravel driveway outside her box-shaped, stucco house.

There was a package on her doorstep. She took it inside with her luggage and closed the door behind her. With the box on the kitchen counter, she unsheathed the SOG blade and cut away the tape. Amid the packing Styrofoam was a high-grade bottle of dark Australian shiraz. She set the bottle in the sink and cracked open the dark glass with the knife. The glass split, still held in place by the thick label, and the wine drained down the sink. From inside the bottle, she retrieved a vacuum-sealed plastic pouch protecting a burner phone. She cut open the plastic and let the air expand around the phone. Her kitchen smelled like a winery now. She turned on the cell phone and saw the single number loaded into the bank. Before dialing the number, she stuffed the wet glass from the bottle into the box with the packing Styrofoam and took it out to her backyard. She had a burn barrel in the center of the dead lawn. Kari got it ready by tossing in four pieces of wood from the chopped pile and a stack of old newspapers. She doused the top with a splash of diesel fuel from the can beside the deck. She put a filtered cigarillo between her lips and lit the tip with a book of hotel matches, then dropped the match into the barrel. When the flames started licking the edges of the barrel and deep black smoke lifted up into a cloudless sky, she threw in the package and called the number.

The phone rang.

She puffed on the Caribbean tobacco.

A familiar voice answered. It was not the voice she had anticipated.

"Didn't think you'd call so soon."

"I just got back. Where's Declan?"

"Declan's here. He's sitting right in front of me."

"And the old man?"

"He's not here."

"Put Declan on the phone."

The voice paused.

"Wouldn't be much point. He can't tell you anything I can't already."

"And who exactly are you?"

"You don't recognize my voice?"

"Vaguely," she said.

"It's Ray."

"Okay, Ray. Ask Declan why I'm a thousand short."

"Declan can't talk."

"Why not?"

"The uh...part of the brain that handles speech and cognition. You know what I mean?"

"No."

"Yeah, that part is dripping down the wall a few feet behind him. A little bit sprayed his computer screen. He's not about to cut anybody a check."

"Then can you explain why I'm short?"

"I'm pulling in the assets we have in the field. You need to come to Boston. Sit down, have a talk. We'll get you paid, and get you caught up."

"Caught up on what?"

"Corporate restructuring."

"I'm not risking my life for a thousand dollars. You didn't want to pay on those contracts, I'll just eat the loss. I don't travel anywhere I don't want to go. I'm independent. Our contract is through."

"Well, it's been decided that we don't work with independent contractors any longer. Liability problems. So you can come see us in Boston and sign an exclusive contract, or somebody can come see you in Virginia. How's that?"

She pitched the phone into the flames.

The sliding glass door to the kitchen was open and, from the backyard, she could hear four heavy knocks at the front of her home followed by the doorbell. She spit out of the cigarillo and drew the Chinese Glock strapped to the bottom of the counter as she approached the front door. Slowly, with the gun raised, she crept closer to the front.

She said nothing.

Two more knocks.

A creak of the floor behind her.

She moved halfway toward the noise and caught the shotgun aimed at her shoulder. A plain-clothes officer with a heavy Kevlar vest had let himself inside through the backyard.

"You're surrounded."

"You watched my car at the airport and followed me home."

"Drop the gun."

She tossed the Glock onto the couch to prevent it from firing.

"On your knees."

She fell to her knees and instinctively interlaced her fingers as she placed them on her head. The rest of the police squad used a battering ram to punch through the locks on the front door. Before she was handcuffed and read her rights, the detectives asked her if there were any active explosives in the house. She was checked for additional weapons and brought into the squad car.

The man who arrested her was tall, black, and wore a pink shirt paired with a purple tie. He had clean, thin dreadlocks that he kept pulled back into a thick ponytail. He stepped inside the interrogation room with a file the size of a phonebook and a stack of compact discs. It was an old cop trick, make it look like they had a mountain of evidence on you.

The walls of the room were white drywall, not the raw cinderblock she had come to expect. Perhaps that was only inside prisons and jails.

"I'm Agent Sanders. You can call me Darius."

"FBI?"

"That's right. But I'm from here. I'm local."

"Didn't make it far from Quantico."

"Didn't have to go far to get there in the first place. My dad was born in Prince William County if you can believe it. Not me, I'm from Richmond."

"I had asked for a drink and a smoke."

He nodded his head.

"Don't worry. It's coming."

He set the files on the table between them and took out a pad of Docket Gold and a heavy fountain pen.

"Can you pronounce your name for me?"

"Kari Jäger. Spelled with a 'j' but said like a 'y.' Two dots above the 'a' if possible."

"Like the drink or the famous pilot."

She nodded.

"It's the same word."

"German?"

"It is."

"Where are you from, Kari?"

"Montana."

The door knocked. The agent got up and cracked open the threshold. He set a gray can of Diet Coke and a pack of Marlboro Menthols with a small tin-foil ashtray in front of her. With her cuffed hands, she placed the can by her side and took out one of the cigarettes. The agent across from her kept the Bic and leaned over to light the cigarette.

"So," he said, sitting down again. "Montana. Must have been beautiful."

"It's a horrible place."

"Is that why you travel so much now?"

She shrugged.

"You don't know?"

She said nothing.

"You travel a lot. There's no reason why you're gone all those weeks?"

She took a drag off the menthol.

He smiled.

"Alright, you know when to keep your mouth shut. That much is clear. But you have to realize, Kari, that I'm not here to establish guilt. It's been well-established. You're a mass murderer."

"No-"

"Don't," he said, interrupting her. "Don't say anything. Just listen to me first."

He pushed the stack of files toward her.

"This isn't a prop. Another thing you need to realize is that I don't need your help. We can find other things you've done. But in terms of prosecuting you, we have more than enough evidence. Whatever you disclose to me today cannot hurt you any more than you have already hurt yourself."

She opened the folder of files and found a photograph of the frozen man in the lawn chair. Upstate Michigan. That was a bad one.

"Louis Quinto," he said. "Inventive in its cruelty. Where did you come up with that?"

She remembered the man had several gambling debts and knew a few secrets about the head of a Waste Management front. They wanted him to suffer. She needed the code to a safe as well. Kari caught up with him at a lake house in the dead of winter. She strapped him naked to a lawn chair in the backyard with duct tape then set the coiled hose in a bucket of warm water to prevent the water from freezing. She hooked the pressure gun to the hose and sprayed the man until his skin was covered in purple and black welts. He froze to death in the chair that night.

"Keeping the hose warm was my idea. But the Pinochet regime had a similar torture method."

"Your father was from Chile, right?"

She nodded.

"It's not how it was done that interests me, Kari. It is why. Aside from robbing these people, why do you do it? Do you like it?"

"I don't like anything I do."

"Then why do it?"

She paused.

"So you don't know everything."

She took a deep breath.

The agent was stoic.

"Fuck it. The guys in Boston were going to kill me anyway. I guess this is what they were trying to prevent, right? Me talking to you? Screw it."

"Guys in Boston?"

"The Mob. At least, what's left of it."

"Let me get this straight. You're saying you work for the mafia?"

"Why do you think I travel so much? I'm a professional."

The agent began to massage his temple.

"Continue," he said.

"Literally, right before you arrested me. I got a call from Boston. My handler was killed and they were about to kill me to shut me up. They could smell something was happening. I think they knew you were on to me."

"And they were going to neutralize you?"

"Of course," she said, tapping the cigarette ash.

The agent pulled back the folder and began combing through pages.

"You said you were talking to these guys in Boston. Give me names."

"My handler is Declan Mahoney. He's dead. There's an old man they call Tosaigh. He's like the Irish version of a Capo. The new head is a guy called Ray. I don't know his last name."

He scribbled the names down and stood up.

"You contacted them on a burner phone, right? Which was mailed to you?"

"Yes."

"Be right back," he said, walking out of the room.

She was alone again. For how long this time, she didn't know. She stubbed out the cigarette in the ashtray. She was impressed they let her smoke. It didn't look like the kind of room where one might be permitted to smoke.

A few minutes went by and she cracked open the can of Diet Coke, taking a short sip before setting it back into the ring of condensation on the plastic table.

The agent returned to the room with another officer holding a laptop. He was white and significantly older.

"Kari, this is agent Binder. You mentioned Quantico. He trains cadets there. He's been assisting us in your case."

"Okay."

They sat down and faced the laptop screen toward her. Darius took a disc from the stack.

"We're gonna show you videos. Then we're gonna talk about what we see."

"Okay."

He placed the disc into the laptop and forwarded through some black and white footage of her Nissan at the parking garage.

"This was four days ago, just before your flight to Tampa. You had just pulled into the garage. You put your ticket on the dash and locked your doors. Do you see that?"

"I see it," she said, taking a sip of Coke.

Binder stopped the tape and spoke for the first time.

"Notice what you're carrying in your hand. It looks like a little file envelope. Do you see it?"

She nodded.

"Notice what happens here."

He played the footage. Her outline disappeared behind the adjacent car. He stopped the video.

"We checked it before you flew in this afternoon. It was full of money. We have the ATM records that show you withdrew it from your own account a day before."

"I don't understand."

"Kari, this Declan Mahoney you said was your Mafia handler? He was a lobbyist from Alexandria who went missing four years ago. The house you've been residing in these past years is still listed as one of his properties."

"We're searching the grounds for his remains," Darius said.

"Postal records show you sending things to yourself. Phones. Money. Instructions written in your own script."

"Your money comes from a trust fund; the rest is stolen from your victims."

"Targets," she said.

"They're victims."

Binder closed the laptop.

"You've been living in a fantasy world."

She stared at the table.

"Do you believe it yourself?"

"What?"

"Do you really think you're an assassin? Or is this also part of your fantasy fulfillment?"

Kari lowered her head.

"I think that's enough for tonight," he said.

COYOTE MAN

Through the window screen, this near-halftone image of an urban bedroom--bathed in muted, incandescent light from the brittle plastic lampshades--exists as a comforting refuge from the monotony of the interstate where at night the long carpets of asphalt lead only to the jarring glare of reflective green signs and short glimpses of an endless wooded void. Hanging back, knees sinking into the thin layer of sod over the clay, face covered by the shadows of rhododendron leaves, he scans the domestic scenery and wonders how long it took to fill this once empty room inside the apartment unit.

The woman enters. She's young, mid-twenties, dark skin, hefty, possibly pregnant. She wears a white negligee and brushes her teeth as she sits on the edge of the mattress.

Is she talking to someone, an invisible husband? Men, with hulking Wal-Mart beef-steak shoulders, who write death warrants with their bare hands, can't always be avoided depending on the house he chooses, or the time of night, or the floorplan. Men linger in living rooms and garages, in basements and backyard shacks, with their beer cans and tools and shotgun racks and rifles...

But she isn't talking to anyone. She's just moving her mouth to facilitate the toothbrush. He can't see the bathroom when she gets up to spit.

He's left with the bedroom again. There's an old movie poster on the wall. It's a film he hasn't seen. His eyes follow the rough patch in the half-assed drywall job--which she's tried to cover up by taping little rectangles of watercolor paper with imitation Picasso works on them--to an open book bag full of textbooks beside a writing desk. She's a student of some kind. She comes back into the frame and gets ready for bed. She peels back the covers and nestles herself into the sheets with the stuffed animals (travel mementos, gifts, and worn childhood favorites alike) then reaches over to the nightstand to turn off the lamp. Christmas lights thumbtacked to the ceiling keep the room alive in a dreamlike semi-glow.

Moving back into the leaves, he sits on the wet ground. Maybe he sees what he's done, or about to do? He's frozen now, etched into the wood engraving of time, which for him is not fluid but dense and organic and compounded many times over into a horrific and indestructible burden. He stares through the dead blackberry thorns at the back alley between the complex and the empty lot at the main road where the stray cats slide out from under the latticed fence draped with interwoven kudzu vine and a single street light shines an icy blue streak on the loose gravel. He sees a world in this alley, a universe, a stage. He's one of many gods of the night. He is this place now.

The dim image in the window is separate from this outer world. It's an ornate work hanging alone in the silence of an alien museum.

A dog enters the room and starts barking at the window. He retreats further into the cover of the leaves. Aggravated, she kicks off the covers and gets out of bed to rein in the yapping fox terrier. He isn't sure if this dog is a fox terrier or some iteration of two or more barn breeds, but its ears are pointed and its snout narrow like a spear. He has a psychic connection with these kinds of dogs due to the coyote in his bloodstream. He rolls up his jean sleeves and crawls out of the bushes like a cave dweller. He takes a seat on the damp concrete of the storm drain, taps a cheap Maverick out of the wrinkled pack, ignites a cardboard match, and scrunches the left side of his face as the smoke pours into his eyes. He exhales a cloud. It stagnates above him like fog.

He leaves his DNA all over the crime scene. It doesn't matter. He's never been fingerprinted. He enters, ghost-like, then bathes in the world he disrupts before continuing along the highway route. If he takes money, he takes cash. When she's gone, her face bruised beyond its original shape, a belt or a phone charger around her neck, legs spread so wide they're dislocated from their sockets, he'll release the yapping dog from the closet. Once its legs are tied to the living-room ceiling fan, he rummages through her kitchen to find the sharpest knife and exsanguinates the terrier. He prepares and eats the gristle-filled cutlets with egg yolk and salsa from her fridge. While drinking a diet Coke, he is inspired by the decor of her bedroom. He draws a coyote on the bathroom mirror with a blue marker.

He spends the afternoon wandering through a drugstore, making the teenage clerks and the middle-aged pharmacist deeply uncomfortable. You can smell him from five feet away. He's gonna buy something, probably a new pack of cheap cigarettes and a bag of beef jerky. He looks at the boutique genetic test kits. He's always wanted to do one of these, but even when he had the money he had no return address. And what would it say anyway? They wouldn't be able to determine anything about him. They'd think it was some kind of joke or contaminated sample. His mother's family came from Oklahoma. That much he knew. Somewhere along the line, they pushed further west into the chaparral and she eventually landed in the raw desert living off of crystal meth and truck-stop prostitution. Her background was never really clear. She had stories about the Tecumseh Rebellion and Jews escaping Hitler and Mexican tequileros during prohibition and West Virginia mountain kin and Tennessean Mulongeons and Irish-Jamaican opium pirates and Gypsy carnival barkers, but nothing to corroborate these fleeting notions. But he had something better than a genetic test. He had the Shaman and the Shaman told him exactly what he was.

He sat alone at the truck stop, ten years old, wrapped in his mother's coat, exhaling clouds of visible breath in the desert-night cold, when the Shaman came and sat next to him on the bench in the dead light of the truck depot while his mother took care of a driver a few yards off.

"You know what you are, boy?" he said in a cold, low rasp. "You know who your daddy is?"

He shook his head. He had never known. His mother didn't have a whimsical answer to fill in that particular gap.

"That's because your mom got raped by a pack of coyotes 'fore she had you. You got the mą'ii in your blood now. You're less than human."

"I ain't no coyote."

The Shaman reached out and smacked him across the face, knocking him to the asphalt.

He didn't know it at the time, but the shaman had given him a gift: the gift of his true identity. He lives his life on instinct, wandering from place to place, knowing there is no question to answer, no goal to be met. His purpose is simply to be. He's free to exist as a wild animal, eater of dog meat.

He pays for a pack of cigarettes and a bag of beef jerky in cash and finally leaves, the staff taking a collective sigh of relief.

GOBLIN MARKET

The wind bent the palmettos outside Joe's window. The unsecured, wooden-slat shutters crashed periodically against the vinyl siding like the discharge from a .22. He sat near the patio door with a glass of bourbon and a Marlboro light in his hand. He wore jeans and a Hawaiian shirt, no socks. The grill cover had torn itself free earlier and sailed down the street. He rocked in the leather office chair and enjoyed the heavy downpour.

Two minutes down the road, Gills Creek had already taken a Subway franchise and a payday loan shark outfit was close to sinking into the water. That's what the radio said before he lost power. Without the radio or the TV, there wasn't much else to do but sit and enjoy the mayhem and get drunk.

He pulled out his phone, which still had data, and turned off the shrill flash flood warning for the sixth time. He took a long drag on the cigarette and let the smoke exit his nostrils. After skimming a few headlines on his news feed, he got up and walked to the kitchen, leaving a thin trail of cigarette smoke in the dark hallway where his face was obscured except for a single red ember bobbing at the vicinity of his phantom lip. A magnolia branch swiped at the window above the sink. He tapped his ash over the garbage disposal and got a beer from the fridge. The overflowing recycling bin sat in the cramped vestibule between the kitchen and the back door facing the driveway. He drained the green bottle of Beck's and flung it at the loaded, bread-smelling bin, knocking loose another bottle. He parted the blinds and saw the foreign car parked behind his black Chevy. A hooded figure braced against the wind and moved up the path toward the front door. He watched as the squat figure took shelter under the eave of this front stoop. A balled fist hammered the door. He took a loaded magnum from the more-or-less empty cabinet drawer and left the kitchen.

He looked through the peephole and saw a girl. She couldn't have been any older than her mid-twenties. A lone strand of her hair had escaped from the bandana beneath the hoodie. The tip was bright pink while the rest was a natural, dark brown. There was an opal stud in her right nostril. Everything about her screamed, "My car has a decal from the university."

She kept knocking.

He pointed the magnum away and cracked the door.

"Can I help you?"

He spoke with a noticeable lisp.

"I'm looking…" was all she managed to say. She stuttered. Her face was red. She appeared to be in the throes of some kind of episode. No one had a good reason to be out in this weather, and there were few reasons anyone came to his front door.

"You're looking," he said. "We're all looking, aren't we?"

"I need to know if this is real. They told me to say something."

"Listen," he said as he tossed the cigarette over her head. "Get back into your car. You clearly don't know what the fuck's going on. If you don't leave right now, I'll call the police."

"Are you Garcia?"

He hesitated.

"I'm sorry, I'm flustered. I've never done anything like this."

"Who's Garcia?"

"I was told to ask for a man called Garcia."

"There's nobody here by that name," he said and slammed the door.

He walked away, returning to the kitchen. He parted the blinds again to watch the girl leave.

She was still there, sitting with her back to the door on the stoop in the pouring rain. It looked like she was sobbing into her hands.

He was drunk.

A violent gust of wind launched a tide of rainwater and debris against the window.

He reached into the fridge and took out one of the last Heinekens. The magnum was stashed in his belt loop behind his back. He unfastened the chain and opened the door to the crying girl. He tapped her shoulder with the green glass and gave her the beer.

"You said it close enough. Get inside."

She stood up feebly and entered. He closed the door behind her.

"You think you can keep it together and tell me what's going on?"

"Yeah, I think I can do that."

"Is your name Garcia?"

"Don't worry about my name. Here, go sit on the couch. I'm gonna get myself another beer."

She stepped into Joe's living room while he took a Beck's for himself.

"The living room smells like ass. Sorry about that," he said from the hall. He went back to the living room and pulled his leather chair away from the French doors.

"So, who and what are you?"

She fidgeted with the Heineken label.

"My name's Shawn," she said.

"Short for Shawna?"

"It's a middle name."

"And your first name?"

"Chrysallis."

"I get it," he said. "Well, what can I do for you, Shawn?"

"I heard you get people back. I heard you get kids back."

"Sometimes," he said.

"I need to get someone back."

"Who?"

"A little boy."

"Where'd he go?"

"I think he's up north, in Charlotte."

"That's not a lead. You think he's in North Carolina? Why do you think that? How old is this boy? What's his name? Has he gone missing? Who is he to you? Do you know who took him? Why? I need you to start over. First, how you heard about the Garcia code, then I need you to explain your story from the beginning, okay?"

She took a deep breath.

"I work for a local food bank."

"Harvest Hope?"

"That's the one," she said. "It's good work."

"If you say so."

She paused to wipe away her tears.

"I do," she said. "It's important work. I've worked there for years but I also mentor kids in an after-school program, or at least I did. The program ended last year. We'd get them some food, help with homework, wait for the folks to pick them up. That sort of thing. And you know, you eventually bond with some of them. You look out for them. You learn who their parents are, even if their parents aren't the good guys."

"As one does," he said, digging another cigarette out of the soft pack on the coffee table, lighting it with the cheap, neon-green Bic. "You're making your way to the boy now. He meant something to you."

"His name's Jibrail Cunningham."

"Black kid?"

"What's it matter?"

"It matters a great deal. I might need to know what he looks like."

"Yeah, he's black. He's short. Here, I got a picture on my phone."

"Don't show it to me yet. Just tell me what happened."

"I still looked out for this kid after the program ended. I knew something was wrong between him and his uncle."

"He was being molested?"

"Something along those lines. But his mom was the bigger problem. She didn't give a shit about this kid one way or the other."

"Shawn," he said. "I'm not a social worker. Just get to the point."

"I go to pick him up after school. He would call me if his uncle didn't show, or if none of his friends could give him a ride. He had my number. He called me to pick him up because his mother had told him he was going away to a boarding school in North Carolina and that a white man with an accent was going to pick him up from school. He asked me to pick him before they took him away. I got there, playing it cool. They said his mother's boyfriend already came and got him."

"Did you ask if he looked stressed, or went with the man willingly?"

"I showed up last. They looked at me like I was suspicious. I had no authority."

"You should have called the police."

"I did. I filed a report and gave them everything."

"Nothing came up?"

"Nothing."

"What about the mom?"

"She overdosed a few weeks later."

"Probably on a binge from the money she made handing him over," he said, scratching his stubble. "What about the uncle?"

"He left town after the police questioned him. I don't think he has anything to do with it. He just didn't want anyone to find out he abused him before all this."

"How did he call you?"

"To come pick him up?"

"Yeah."

"School phone."

Joe took a drag on the cigarette.

"Why do you think he's in Charlotte?"

"He said so. That's where the boarding school was supposed to be."

"That's better than nothing."

She hesitated and peeled the label completely free from the bottle.

"So can you find him?"

"How did you hear about me?"

"People we help at work. Maybe a drug dealer or two."

"What'd they say?"

"They said you're an ex-UN translator, that you move in bad circles and that you're one of the best."

"I'm going to tell you what I tell everyone."

She looked ready.

"He's probably dead."

"I know."

"Give me the money."

She pulled a wad of cash out of her bag and handed it to him.

"That's nineteen-hundred dollars."

He counted it.

"Dead or alive, you're not getting this back."

"I know."

"That's what they all say when they still have hope."

"Do you have any hope?"

"I'm still doing this, aren't I?"

From a motel room outside Greenville, South Carolina, Joe called an Episcopal Church and asked for a Father Winter, saying he was an old friend from the DRC and that his name was Joe Merci. A few minutes later, a deep voice answered the line.

"Hey, Joe. Been a long time since Kinshasa. How are you?"

"Parking garage just off Main. 9 pm."

"Yeah, breakfast sounds great. I'll bring the Mrs."

"Find out what you can about Charlotte these days."

"Alright, buddy. We'll catch up then. Tell her I said 'hi.'"

Joe hung up.

He was at the top of the parking garage inside his car because the rain wouldn't stop. He had a different gun, an automatic Sig Sauer, shoved in his coat pocket. A cigarette hung from his lip but he refrained from lighting it. He played with a stainless-steel Zippo as he waited for the priest. The curved lamp posts ate into the night sky like black fishhooks. The light from their dark, orange bulbs changed the hue of the beige concrete to a warm gold and the rain sometimes looked like dying sparks.

A gray Honda Element pulled up against his black Chevrolet. He unlocked the doors.

Father Winter, wearing an enormous Northface jacket, jetted from the front seat of his Honda and, through the rain, slid into the shotgun seat beside Joe.

"You didn't have to call the office."

"I had to get rid of your number last time."

"Who's the lucky lady?"

He shook his head.

"Twelve-year-old boy."

"Ouch. How much?"

"Not enough."

"Then why?"

"Because."

"Yeah, I got you. Here," he said, handing Joe a leather wallet. "Don't worry, it's got aluminum inserts to bounce off any RFID signals."

"Who am I?"

"You're a caseworker from Orangeburg. Name is Harlan Hammersleigh."

Joe looked at the forged I.D.

"That's a stupid name."

"Well, he's dead. Social security card is in there too."

Joe pocketed the wallet.

"What do you know about Charlotte?"

"I know the Super Bowl is over."

"What happened after Craigslist?"

"There's a little place where people drink and play cards. It's a tiny building close to North Davidson between a donut place and a bus stop. The address is in the wallet. It might look like someone's garage annex. You gotta know who to know if you want to play. It's that kind of deal."

"What? They play cards and fuck kids. Is that it?"

"It took me a long time to find these guys. The forum was pretty deep. It's like an auction house. The pot is the victim. The buy-in covers the cost."

"The cost? This isn't like 'I work at a preschool' or take the nephew home for the weekend kind of shit. They're purchasing them straight from people in the trade?"

"At least one of them is. Whoever is organizing it."

"You're sure this address is good?"

"I did my best."

"We'll see."

"I'm gonna go now."

"Alright."

"Let me know when you need a passport again."

"I'll be seeing you, Winter."

"I bet you will. Let me ask you something in earnest. You ever think about Congo and wonder if we really ever left?"

"I'll see you around."

"Yeah, I'll see you."

He slammed the door shut.

He left Greenville in the morning with his new identity and an uncertain lead. Charlotte wasn't far. He got in early and checked into a shabby room at a meth den called the Executive

Inn. He lay his back flat on the edge of the mattress and stared at the ceiling and thought about nothing.

He found a bar and started drinking in the middle of the day. He had a few shots of Bourbon and five beers before settling his tab. He wiped the edges of the glass and bottles with an alcohol swab. There was a taco truck across the street in a near-vacant gravel lot. He sat at a picnic table and ate tacos and an empanada. He crushed the paper plates and napkins into a ball of tin foil and threw it away in a back alley dumpster. When he got back to the room, he started draining plastic bottles of spring water he'd bought at a drugstore to back the booze. He took a sleeping pill and went to bed in the late afternoon.

He woke up the next morning at 4:30 am. He brushed his teeth in the bathroom while staring at the mirror in the weak light and put on his clothes in the dark. Before leaving, he kept the door ajar and placed the do-not-disturb sign on the outside, and then took the large, green-metal thermos from his bag. He made sure the door was locked; the room key was secure in his new wallet. He wiped the handle with an alcohol swab. The motel smelled like cigarettes and butane. He wore a black jacket zipped all the way to his chin, khaki pants, and black tennis shoes. His thermos looked like a core sample in his hand. It was early enough that he could see the residue of nightmares and certain dreams calcifying on the walls. The hallway appeared like a grid with plenty of space between the lines. It was in that space he could almost reach out his hand and touch the hidden texture of death. It was a texture he hadn't felt in years, but when he did, it was familiar to him. He had felt it on the tips of his fingers and toes as a teenager sick with the flu. Some of his earliest memories in the crib were bathed in this strange texture. The sensation came and went throughout the years. Today was an odd day to feel it. He let it wash over him and disintegrate as he entered the front lobby.

The man at the reception desk was slumped over the counter in the flicker of the TV screen, snoring. Joe drank a few cups of water from the cooler and filled his thermos with coffee.

He drove north on the highway toward a mirage of lights and tall buildings. It was still dark out as the first sign of dawn sat just beneath the horizon like a slow-building fire in the distance. There were hundreds of cars on the road. He hit the ramps of the urban center and came closer to his target. He left the skyscrapers behind, cruising underneath railroad bridges until he found himself on the narrow streets of an adjacent borough.

He found the corner at Dunkin' Donuts and the bus stop. Past the chainlink on the opposite end of the street, he could see the squat garage annex beside the narrow, somewhat out-of-place New-England-style home wedged inside the decrepit neighborhood clutter. It had a small backyard with a privacy fence from which a centuries-old elm tree's gnarled branches protruded, tapping the attic window, raking the gutters. He parked up the street in front of a derelict home and watched the house and garage in his rearview mirrors.

At 7:30 am, lights inside the house started turning on. There were two windows he could see: a downstairs kitchen and what he assumed was a bathroom on the higher floor. He sipped coffee and turned on the radio. When he had to pee, he walked across the street to the Dunkin' Donuts. He knew some private investigators who had so many bad experiences trying to piss in used bottles and cups on hotel stakeouts that they eventually invested in disposable plastic bladders with special one-way flow nozzles that fit the head of the penis. He couldn't imagine using something like that.

He bought two sandwiches and ate one outside before getting back in the car. 8:30 came around and he watched a tall man with blonde hair and thin glasses leave the house. There was a door on the side of the garage. He unlocked it and stepped through. The large garage door stayed shut. Joe bet he never opened it. The blonde guy came out with a mountain bike and locked the side door behind him. Joe was right. He kept watching as the man lifted the bike over the waist-high chain link and pedaled down the road.

Joe waited. He knew the man would only be gone for a moment since he had no backpack or some kind of briefcase bag over his shoulder. He cracked the window and pulled the plastic off a new hard pack of Marlboro Lights. He tapped it against the steering wheel, peeled back the foil, and took out a cigarette. He smoked it as he studied the neighborhood coming to life like a rusted gear steadily cranking into full rotation. A few women sat down by the bus stop. A big guy in sweatpants and a sweatshirt opened up the gate and took a seat on the concrete step at the end of the way. Joe monitored the house to see if there was any more activity. Things looked still but he couldn't be sure.

The blonde man sailed back down the street on his bike. He had a supermarket bag balanced on the handlebars. He took his groceries inside. Joe crushed out the cigarette and lit the opposite end of the filter. The cellulose acetate melted as the paper ignited. He stepped out of the car and stamped it out with the treadless sole of his tennis shoes and then walked to the end of the block. The big guy in the sweatshirt gave him a slight nod of acknowledgment. Joe returned the gesture.

"What's good?"

"It's all good."

"You smoke?"

"Yeah."

Joe offered him a cigarette.

"Nah, I'm good."

"Cool."

Joe lit another for himself.

"How much you know about this block?"

"I don't know much."

Joe handed him forty dollars.

He reached into his pants and gave him a baggie full of Oxycontin.

"No, you keep it. I just wanna know about the house. You know anything about that place?" he said, pointing to the garage.

The big guy took a quick glance down the street as he pocketed the baggie.

"You a cop?"

"No, I'm like a PI."

"You got a PI license."

"No, I said I'm *like* a PI. I'm just looking for somebody."

"Oh, you lookin' for somebody."

"It isn't like that. I'm not gonna kill anyone. I'm just try-ing to make sure somebody's safe is all."

"That's all you fixin' to do?"

"That's it."

"Maybe you should be thinkin' about killing somebody then, if you all on the up and up like you say. Know what I'm sayin'? 'Cause that place down there ain't no fuckin' joke."

"What do you mean?"

"I mean, you seen that motherfucker come out there ridin' his bike to the co-op like he's Mr. Rogers and shit. That's all make-believe. You feel me?"

"I figured as much."

"Matter fact, kids don't go trick-or-treatin' to that house anymore. At least, that's the rumor."

"Shit," Joe said and took a drag.

"It's fucked up."

"Appreciate the tip. Anybody asks, we didn't have this conversation."

"Who would come up here askin'?"

"Probably nobody."

Joe walked back to the car and pulled a u-turn. He parked up the street beside the sidewalk and privacy fence to the back-yard with the elm. He wouldn't be able to see Blondie leave the front door but he might catch a glimpse of him crossing the street with his bike. Now that he had come and gone once, Joe couldn't let him see his car again. There was a single win-dow beside the patio door. He could see half of it above the fence; only able to make out a short ceiling. Was it a hallway? He didn't know, but he could see the light from the kitchen. He took out his binoculars and focused on the smoke detector in the sideways glare from the stove lamp.

At 9:00 am, the light switched off. Two minutes later, Blondie crossed the street on his bike with a brown leather satchel strapped across his shoulder. Joe watched the house a little longer. He saw no one else. The coast was clear. He popped the trunk and stepped out onto the sidewalk. After checking the street and determining he was alone, he set the Sig Sauer in his jacket pocket, pulled on his work gloves, and took out the crowbar from beneath the spare tire. He used the crowbar to pry two picket boards loose from the fence and leaned them in place to cover the gap once he had entered the yard. Before he approached the garage, he checked the opposite street to make sure he was alone. He took the crowbar in both hands and struck the doorknob until it was free. The warped brass handle and exposed lock mechanism dropped to the ground. He pried the rest of the door frame apart, pulling two more locks out of the now splintered wood, and kicked the door open.

He hit the lights. The interior was covered in gray carpet. Three soundproofing panels were mounted on the far wall, the metal exterior of the large garage door. There was a mini-fridge plugged into an outlet beside the green-felt poker table. The metal shelf had different equipment for bicycle maintenance and a metal suitcase. Joe opened the suitcase. It was just a case for the poker chips. He walked around the room. He felt the walls to see if there might be a seam for a deliberate tear. There wasn't.

He sat down at the table and opened a deck of cards. He spread them, face-up, across the table, then checked the mini-fridge. It was filled with cans of German pilsner and a few Coca-Colas. He checked the freezer cabinet above the cans where he found a plastic bag. He unwrapped the Ziploc and let three frozen solid burner phones fall onto the table.

The back door to the yard slammed shut.

Joe tossed away the bag and picked up the crowbar. He could hear footsteps frantically racing toward the garage. The blonde man whimpered as he saw the debris from the forced entry. Joe hid behind the open door. Without hesitation, the young man crossed the threshold to see what had been stolen.

Joe closed the door as much as possible.

The blonde man whipped around and yelled in shock.

"Don't move," Joe said, pointing the crowbar at him.

"The fuck are you?"

"I'm not a burglar. I'm not police either. Do what I say, you won't get hurt. Take a seat."

He sat down.

"There's no money here for you to steal."

"We both know I'm not here to steal money," Joe said. "What's your name?"

"I'm not gonna give you my name."

"I can find out. I know your face."

"And I know yours," he said.

"You'll wish you didn't. I'm gonna call you Blondie, okay?"

He didn't respond. He looked meek, panicked.

"Blondie, you need to listen to everything I say. Most people who see their doors broken into like that call the cops first.

Not you. You're hiding something, something no one is supposed to see. I know what is. I'm not a vigilante. I'm not going to expose you. I'm not going to kill you. I have one purpose. Get someone back. That's all I'm here to do."

He was silent.

Joe took his phone from his pocket. He kept his eyes on him as he pulled up a picture of the boy.

"Look at this. You see it. Do you recognize him?"

"I've never seen him before."

"Look again. Look at it. You look at them all the time on your own and now you're afraid to put your eyes on him?"

He stared at the picture.

"You know this kid. Right?"

He said nothing.

"I'm not a cop. This isn't an elaborate scheme to get you to confess. I don't care who you bought him from, or for how much. I just want to know where he is."

His eyes darted around the room. He noticed the phones on the table. He focused on Joe and the crowbar.

"I can see you're thinking about rushing me. One guy with an iron. How hard could it be?"

Joe leaned on the crowbar like a cane and took out the pistol.

"Who won the game? Come on."

"I don't know where he lives. I don't know his real name."

"Yes, you do. Rules of the buy-in. You have to have collateral on the players."

He gritted his teeth.

"Shit," he said.

"Blondie, it's a lot harder to tell me things with a bullet in your knee cap."

"Shane Nuback: 1411 College Street, Rock Hill."

Joe dropped the crowbar and pressed on it with his foot to secure it as he took out his phone and plugged in the address. It was real.

"Alright. Not too far from here, huh?"

"No. It's not far away. I can call him and he'll give him back to you."

Joe shot him in the stomach. Smoke lingered in the air between them. The smell of cordite filled the garage. Blood pooled around his abdomen. His expression didn't change. Joe fired again, this time at his head. His neck jerked backward. A streak of dark blood and skull fragments splashed across the poker table. His body went limp and slid onto the floor.

Joe picked up the shell casings and his crowbar. He walked outside. Birds rustled through the trees, disturbed by the muted gunshots. The street was empty. He walked through the backyard to the opening he made in the fence. He set the picket boards in place and returned to the trunk where he set the crowbar back underneath the spare tire and peeled off his work gloves. There was a secret compartment on the left where he stuffed the gloves, the pistol, and his spent shell casings. He whistled as he closed the trunk and got back inside the Chevy.

The house was large and covered in gray-vinyl siding. The driveway faced the main road. The front door was connected to the sidewalk by a narrow brick path behind a row of sticker bushes and cypress trees. There were a few law firms and a YMCA nearby, but most of the real estate belonged to upper-class homes.

Joe pulled into the driveway. He took the Sig Sauer from the compartment in the trunk after putting on his gloves. He stepped past the AC unit and meter into the grass along the side of the house, making his way to the backyard. He checked the corner at the sunroom and crouched down by the window pane. He could see the living room or some kind of den. The TV was on and tuned into a college football game. A middle-aged white male lounged in the recliner. He was alone.

Joe backed away. He sat down in the grass, his back to the gray vinyl. There was no basement. He could tell that much. He needed to know the lay of the land better and then he could think. He circled the house twice, taking note of any possible exits or entry points. He could sneak inside or he could ring the doorbell and force him by gun-point. There was always the possibility Blondie had lied. He had let guys in Blondie's situation live before to dire consequences. Someone like him would alert his target. It was already on his mind when he offered to make a call for Joe. People did stupid and desperate things when they knew he was coming for them. But the necessity of surprise came with an element of uncertainty. He saw a high win-dow on the opposite end of the house close to the trees. There was a single window partially hidden from the tips of the cypresses. The glass appeared tinted, blocked out by a dark curtain or trash bag.

He got back inside the car and drove away.

He returned an hour later and parked in the empty lot near the law firm. He took the ladder he had purchased at Lowe's out of the back seat and walked across the street. He entered the yard through the bushes and trees and extended the ladder, propping it against the base of the window. He climbed up and took out a brand new glass cutter. He reached his hand through the hole he had carved, flipped the locks, and opened the window. There was an alarm sensor on the frame. It didn't sound. Mr. Nuback had disarmed the security system, probably in the morning. If he had the kid, he wasn't paranoid about it. Joe pushed through the blackout curtain, crawling into the room. It was empty except for a few dusty computer printers lining the wall and some neglected gym equipment. The TV was still on full volume. The noise of the football game carried throughout the house. He left the room and crossed the railed catwalk by the grand stairwell to the guest bathroom and opened the bedroom door. The bedroom was unoccupied. He remembered a windowless four-by-four concrete room outside Matadi close to the Angolan border. He let the memory fade as he searched the bedroom. There were two pillows on the unmade bed. Both had imprints. He checked the master bathroom. There were no tampons in the cabinet, no razors in the shower, no curling iron, no blow dryer, no sign of a woman. He had more than one toothbrush. Joe opened the medicine cabinet and saw three boxes of condoms and a tube of Astroglide. He closed the medicine cabinet and stared at his face.

He checked the closets and the spare bathroom. There was an attic space in the ceiling but he wouldn't pull it down. The unused springs and neglected hinges would make too much noise. Instead, he crept down the stairs and moved through the dining room to the garage. The garage was clean. He had a Ford SUV and an old Dodge Challenger. Abandoning the garage, he went ahead to the living room and stood behind Shane as he watched the Carolina game.

He pressed the barrel of the pistol against his temple.

"What's the score?"

He raised his hands in surrender and began to hyperventilate.

"Put your hands down. I want 'em flat on the armrests."

He lowered them.

"Breathe, Shane."

"You know my name," he managed to say between breaths. He said it as a fact, not as a question.

"Where's Jibrail?"

"I can pay you to keep this quiet. I can give you whatever you want."

"Your poker friend, the Jeffery-Dahmer-looking asshole?"

"I'll tell you where he is."

"I already know where he is. He gave *you* up."

"What did he pay you?"

"Nothing. He's dead."

He started to cry. His lips trembled. His body shook.

"Do you want to die, Shane?"

He burst into tears. Snot dripped down his chin.

"Where's the kid?"

"I have a room between here and the garage."

"Open it up."

"You can't open it from the outside."

He pressed the pistol harder against his head and reached into his lap for the remote to turn off the TV.

"Are you trying to fuck with me?"

He shook his head.

"No, please. Just give me a second. Watch," he said and cleared his throat. "Jibrail, come out here."

Joe watched as the bookcase lifted from the wall and swung forward as the boy pushed with both hands. He hesitated as he limped into the living room. The right side of his face was swollen and purple. Joe couldn't avert his eyes. He was starving. He could sequester himself from Shane for days inside the fortified room, but he didn't eat unless he did what he said.

"Jibrail?"

The boy nodded.

"Shawn sent me. I'm here to take you back."

He shook his head.

"You have to believe me."

Shane turned and wrestled Joe to the carpet. He forced the gun from his hand and strangled his throat. Joe's arms were too short to reach up and take hold of anything vital. He scratched at his face and eyelids. Shane was still crying as he pressed his weight on Joe's slim throat.

"I can't let you do this. I'm sorry. You don't know what it's like."

Joe's right hand fell back and flailed in search of the pistol. He struggled to take in a breath.

"I'm so sorry. No one can know."

Joe's eyes rolled back to see the pistol at the boy's feet. He motioned with his hand, asking him for the gun. The boy kicked it forward. It was still a foot away from his grasp.

Shane looked up and scrambled for the weapon.

Joe took in a massive breath and pulled him back across the carpet, sticking his thumb in his eye.

"No!" he yelled, fighting through the pain.

They traded punches.

Joe pushed himself forward and took hold of the pistol.

Shane grabbed his wrist and the gun discharged through his jaw.

Joe fired again. The second round split open his skull, collapsing his face.

His body twitched and dropped to the side as Joe kicked it away. He caught his breath as the boy stared at him.

He assumed a fake identity, always a caseworker or some kind of social services official, for the journey back. That was only if he found the kid. He hadn't been questioned by a police officer in a long time. It was easier to get back with a teenage girl, especially if her age was unclear. But, to his surprise, no one seemed to notice or care what a late-thirties white man was doing with a beaten-up black child in his car.

"Can you get me something to eat?"

Joe reached into the side console and gave him the breakfast sandwich.

"Can I have McDonald's?"

"I'm sorry. I can't stop until we get to Shawn."

"Why not?"

"Because people are going to wonder what you're doing in my car?"

"Just tell them you're good. Tell them you came to get me."

"The world doesn't work that way. You think they'll believe me? Come on, you're twelve years old. You're smarter than that."

"What's your name?"

"I don't have one."

The kid took a bite of the sandwich.

"Are you taking me back to my mom?" he said with his mouth full.

"No, I told you I'm taking you to Shawn. Your mother's dead."

"Good," he said.

They drove for an hour. He took the first exit outside the city and drove past the military base toward the swollen creek. The damage from the hurricane and flooding was evident everywhere he looked. Buildings sloped into the contaminated water. Power lines drooped over the sidewalks. The streets were still littered with torn branches. He pulled into the apartment complex and parked at the top of the hill. They got out of the car and followed the winding path through the tufts of elephant grass to Shawn's door. He knocked.

She pulled open the door and fell to her knees, embracing the boy. Both of them cried.

"You better let the police know you found him," Joe said, standing over them.

"What do I tell them?"

"You tell them he knocked on your door and that was it. Sooner you do it, the better."

They kept crying.

"I'm gonna go now. Don't ever contact me again."

He walked away.

The next day, Joe pulled into his driveway, passing the unmarked cruiser parallel to his mailbox. Detective Haines stood on his front step wearing a white shirt and red tie. He had his gun and his badge on his belt. Joe got out of the Chevy and opened the passenger door for his grocery and liquor store bag.

"You here in official capacity?"

Haines didn't answer him at first.

"How are you doing?" he eventually said. "I was just about to give up on waiting for you."

"I wish you had."

"You doing some shopping?"

He held up the two bottles of bourbon in the black bag.

"Just the essentials."

"You're gonna kill yourself, Joe. What's the point of transitioning if you don't want to be here?"

"Why don't you get to the fuckin' point, asshole?"

"Hippie girl reports a missing kid a while back. She ain't kin or nothing like that. Just lookin' out for him. Some kind of mentorship program. She came in yesterday with the kid. Says he showed up on her doorstep."

Joe set the bags down and tapped a cigarette from the pack.

"Now, I know for a fact you're not supposed to smoke on hormone pills."

"Is that why your daughter quit?" Joe said.

"Part of it, yeah"

"Well, T lowers your life expectancy anyway," he said as he lit the cigarette.

"I didn't know you were still working."

"Does it look like I'm working?"

"Where have you been the last couple of days?"

"Sitting in my house watching the storm."

"Anyone able to corroborate that?"

"Chinese delivery guy. Didn't get his name. Maybe, you can ask him why they botched my order, switched my chicken with beef."

Detective Haines shook his head, smiling.

"You smooth fuck face. How the hell do you do it?"

"By not doing a goddamn thing. You can leave now."

"My daughter says you haven't been to group in a long, long time. You should come by. It's good for you."

"You like saying that, don't you? 'My daughter.' But you say it like you don't believe it."

Detective Haines said nothing and walked across the weed-infested lawn to his car.

LUELLA

Luella Herrera-Reízapal left the state of Indiana after her ex-boyfriend was successfully captured by Interpol. A regional ICE task force arrested him on the rickety front steps of their mobile home. Anton Dubromiović, a tall, physically imposing man despite being twenty years her senior, who drove a Venture Logistics truck for the past eleven years, was not a Croatian refugee. The older man she had lived with, cooked for, taken beatings from, and slept beside for the past thousand nights, was a wanted Serbian war criminal named Alosj Dalek. She packed her things, called the restaurant where she washed dishes, and drove south in the battered, dark-blue Ford Bronco. There were no more Eastern-European football matches on the television. No open-handed slaps in exchange for sarcasm. No more piss-poor Spanish. No Black and Mild cigars. No Vodka. No Jägermeister. No more threats of battery acid.

But she was not free.

"When you have anywhere to go, you have nowhere to go," her brother had said years ago in Ciudad Acuña.

She could sustain herself for a little while on her savings and the thick wad of emergency cash she took from behind the medicine cabinet. She would need work. She could find that easy enough. She was good at getting jobs. Finding a place to stay wherever she ended up would be the real challenge.

She had started in Chicago and, a year later, moved down to Indiana. She had chosen Chicago for the established Mexican presence, and New York City seemed overwhelming. She didn't mind the cold either. She wanted those snowy Christmases from the television specials. It didn't take long to acclimate to the razor-like wind on her cheeks, but her time there was brief. She left for what she perceived to be the fields of the country in the next state over after her apartment building was condemned and the owner of the bodega where she stocked shelves was burned to death in a back-alley dumpster. She moved on to work in soy fields, apple orchards, and a few tree farms, then a temporary warehouse position. She became familiar with the truck drivers and eventually met Anton. He was older but she was attracted to his work ethic and his guidance. They were both immigrants. He looked at her as just one person, one woman who chose to leave home, where other white men saw her as a symptom of a sociopolitical dilemma. She thought of the kids held in detention camps in the Southwest and the raids in Mississippi, then thought of the full-color images she had once seen of starving Bosnian men in concentration camps. Anton had a golden scorpion tattooed on his shoulder framed by a red, white, and blue military patch. He said it referenced a German rock band from the 80s, that he had it done as a kid after a concert.

Luella stopped for coffee once she made it to Kentucky. There was an angular building just off the exit with a large stucco coffee pot sculpture in the gravel driveway. She got out and stretched her legs. The weedy lawn before the steps of the coffee house was littered with folk-art silhouettes and whirligigs. She went inside and struggled to close the door in the wind. There was no one at the register near the chalkboard menus and only one customer sitting in the very back in the dark. Luella stood in silence, pretending to study the menu when the girl in the back yelled out to her in Spanish.

"Are you looking for work? Because there's no work here!"

The girl had a Mexican accent.

"I just want a coffee."

"Sure you do," she said, then yelled to the back for someone to help her.

A white guy emerged from the kitchen and began to shake his head.

"We don't need nobody right now," he said in English.

"I just want a coffee," she said.

"You don't have to buy something just because you came in...it don't make no difference."

She turned around and walked back into the wind.

"Don't come back," she heard the man say through the door.

She drove another eight miles and stopped at a McDonald's. The light was warm inside, the interior newly renovated. She took a seat next to the bathroom and drank her coffee. Two kids ran through the indoor playset on the opposite end of the glass. They were without any visible chaperones. She watched them play as she finished her coffee, inventing a bleak narrative for them. There had been an old barnhouse in the field across from the gas station beside the McDonald's. She imagined they lived there with their father and mother and this McDonald's indoor play place was the only playground in the area and it was safer than playing in the barn with the animals and equipment. Or they had been abandoned by a young mother who could no longer take care of them and hoped this state's welfare system was their best chance at life. She looked at every face in the McDonalds to see who might resemble the little boy and girl.

She turned toward the parking lot where she saw a tall, young man looking through the window of the Bronco at her belongings. He wore multiple layers of shirts to fight the cold above his scuffed jeans. She ran outside when he began jimmying the handle of the Bronco with a metal shim.

"Hey you, get the fuck away from the truck."

It still didn't feel like the truck was hers.

The kid glanced at her with bloodshot eyes.

"This is your truck?"

"Yeah, it's mine," she said. "Get out of here, or I'll call the police."

"Alright," he said, putting the shim in his pocket, backing away from her.

She took out her keys and unlocked the door. As she climbed into the front seat, the kid ran behind her and smashed her face into the steering wheel. He was incredibly weak. She instinctively kicked him in the groin, then turned around and pushed him to the asphalt where she stomped his face. His nose cracked and blood drained down his lips. An old man in a windbreaker ran into the parking lot.

"I saw the whole thing, asshole. You just assaulted this woman."

He had his phone in his hand.

Luella made eye contact with the old man.

"I need to leave," she said.

"Are you okay, Ma'am?"

"Yeah, I'm fine. He didn't hurt me."

"He tried to."

The kid got up and ran.

"Where are you going, asshole? The police are coming. Oh, God damn it."

He punched in 911 on his phone again.

Luella got back into the truck and pulled out of the parking lot.

"Why are you leaving. Don't you want to press charges?"

She didn't say anything as she drove away.

She drove further south through Kentucky, admiring the even green pastures and muscle-bound thoroughbreds galloping along the white fences. In the night, she crossed into the mountains of East Tennessee, took the first exit she saw, and checked into a cheap room. The motel was built next to an old mining quarry. The view from her window was blocked off by a wall of solid rock.

She checked out in the morning. It was the first time in several days she had seen any sunshine. The lack of cloud cover left the terrain vulnerable to frigid, winter-like cold. She could see her breath as she crossed the parking lot. A couple argued in the middle of the street. They both looked feral to her.

Luella had learned to drive on long, straight roads in flat expanses of desert and, later on, thin stretches of gray road bisecting the cornfields. She wasn't used to the winding mountain highway and found herself driving, white-knuckled, non-stop, through the state of Tennessee only to catch her breath once she arrived in North Carolina. Her tires were white from the leftover salt and grit. She bought a map of the state in the evening and spread it across the dashboard. Instead of continuing south, she would head east. She wanted to see the coast. The mountains disappeared behind her as rolling foothills gave way to terrain so flat it looked nearly level. She passed RV dealerships and squat ranch homes built in the shadows of low-hanging billboards on the side of the endless highway. For the first time since leaving Indiana, the radio started picking up Spanish-language stations. It was all *Reggaeton* or *Maria-chi*. Perhaps if she searched hard enough, she might find some *Narcocorrido*, which she abhorred, but nothing as quaint as a *ranchera* or South American *Nueva canción*.

She followed the signs for a coastal town called Beau-fort. Tourist destinations had the most fly-by-night jobs to go around. As the night approached, an influx of warm air spread across the region. Lighting struck in the distance where the faded sky turned black. It was time to find another place to sleep. Her options were sparse. She began to suspect there was nothing between here and the coast.

A light in the distance just beyond the next road sign caught her eye. A young man sat on top of a camping bag with a Coleman lantern by his feet in the sparse weeds. He wore a straw hat and suspenders with his beaten-up clothing. Beside his camping bag, sat a sinister-looking black case with bronze buckles and a firm handle. She imagined he could fit a rifle inside. He had a cardboard sign on his lap: "Oak Island-bound, show to play. Folk-singer. Two or three miles helps."

Luella killed the radio and slowed the car.

The young man smiled.

She stopped, checked the rearview mirror, and idled the Bronco.

"You headed to the coast, Ma'am?"

"I am."

"Oak Island by any chance. I'm a musician. I have a show to play in a few days."

"I don't know Oak Island. I'm going to Beaufort."

She realized she didn't know how to pronounce the name of the town.

"Oh, I see," he said. "Well, that's a different way. See, I'm headed south past Wilmington and you're going way up there past Jacksonville. I don't want to put you out of your way."

He tipped his beaten straw hat to her.

She found the bizarre, arcane gesture slightly disarming.

"I don't have a plan. I chose Beaufort on a map. I'm looking for work. Does Oak Island have tourists?"

"I suppose it does. People only live there part of the year. But the summers are always packed."

She hesitated.

"Well, I guess I can take you."

His face lit up.

"Alright."

He went back to the road for his things, turned off the lantern, and grabbed the black case.

She stopped him in his tracks.

"I need to know what's inside that," she said.

He lifted the case.

"This right here? It's my banjo."

"Show it to me."

He set everything else down and opened up the case. The instrument was worn around the head with flecks of the drum skin eaten away from years of playing, but the fretboard was clean with an elaborate pattern of mother-of-pearl etched into the red wood. He had the case open toward her for her to see there was nothing else hidden inside and began to play a classical roll to show off his skill.

"Okay," she said. "Put your stuff in the back."

He loaded up his things in the back seat and sat beside her as she resumed her journey. The weather finally hit them and she had the windshield wipers on full capacity.

"Good thing you came along when you did," he said.

"I guess you were lucky."

"I suppose I was," he said. "My name's Ford Nix."

"Luella," she said.

"Mucho gusto, Luella."

"You speak Spanish?"

"Nope. Just what I forgot from my school days. I wish I did."

"My English could be better," she said.

"Your English sounds fine to me."

When they passed the storm, the earth around them was pitch black. She was tired and her eyes began to drift. Ford grabbed the wheel and straightened the Bronco as she came to.

"Whoa now," he said. "You gettin' tired?"

"I guess I am."

"You guess. No offense, but I'd like to live to play my show. How far have you come today?"

"I drove in from Tennessee."

"Oh, my God. Do you want me to drive?"

"No," she said. "There's a Coke in the side thing here."

He handed her the warm Coca-cola.

She took a sip.

"You know what you could do," she said.

"Yeah?"

"You could play me some songs. Pay your way to the island."

He reached into the backseat and took out his banjo.

"This is an old-school song I learned when I played out in Texas," he said. "I think it originally had a Spanish title but the white folks on the plains gave it a new name and some English lyrics to go along. They call it *Mexican Banjo*."

He proceeded to play a typical *corrido* along with a twangy mountain wail. His voice filled the cabin of the Bronco and kept her awake. He played all night until they reached Wilmington and slept in a parking lot beside the beach.

A DARK BRASS PAIL

In my dream, Willie Nelson asked me for a glass of wine. He was visiting my modest home (even in dreams I'm poor and complacent about it) to play poker with Emanuel, a co-worker of mine who was also my last remaining black friend ever since the doors of the university had permanently closed on me. My home was covered in flowers but, in the strange tunnel vision the dream afforded me, I couldn't see what kind they were. I only remember an airbrushed, magenta blur covering the small cottage. Everyone and everything seeped into my dreams and, most of the time, I could wake up and recognize the people and the places my subconscious had sewn together, discombobulated, and otherwise edited for time and content. I asked Mr. Nelson if he wanted white or red wine.

"White," he said, without looking at me, tossing in a chip with an almost mechanical second nature; a suave indifference toward the pile in the middle of the table.

I went back to the old kitchenette, hoping there was more than just Bordeaux, bourbon, and beer in my dream fridge, and felt my spirit lift when a cheap bottle of Pinot Gris had transported its way into my visions. All I had in the cupboard were plastic glasses but it didn't matter since they were shaped like traditional wine glasses, fancy ones. I brought the glass back to Willie Nelson feeling greatly accomplished. In most dreams reading a sign, or finding a train station, or dialing 911 often degenerated into cinematic drama marked by physical dysfunction, and failure. He took one look at the drink and said, "Naw, you can leave the pitcher." So I left the glass on the poker table and went back to find a pitcher, but I had no pitcher. Instead, I cleaned out a brass watering pail, carefully scrubbing the edges in the sink, and poured the remainder of the bottle inside. Nelson accepted the vessel without question and I couldn't believe my success. The dream disintegrated into short bursts of unrelated ideas with the poker game as the focal point, the way dirty bathwater circles a drain.

I woke up and thought about the dream and all the things I knew existed in reality. I had a bottle of Pinot Gris that belonged to my girlfriend in the fridge. Emanuel, completely silent throughout the dream, happened to be the best Holdem player I knew, and I had played exchange students from Macau. I wasn't sure why Willie Nelson was in my dream. I didn't listen to his music but I did work with a guy named Willy who sorted through rotten produce at the grocery store. The day before he had talked a lot (too much actually) about lucid dreaming.

I stood up from the bed and parted the shabby curtains. Nothing but brittle forest and sawgrass appeared through my only window in the bottom-floor apartment. In the summer,

I caught a glimpse of a black bear rummaging through the brambles, but that too might have been a dream. I always took a walk before driving to work. The long-neglected sidewalk was chipping away beneath my feet and it worsened every year. Massive roots from the elms pushed up jagged slabs of concrete that were too high for some to stride across. The kudzu had repossessed a third of the pathway and, at the far end only a few yards from the tracks, the entire thing collapsed into ruin like broken pottery scattered in a field. The prevailing segments connected several low-income apartment complexes and ran parallel to the backyards of a cluster of ranch homes. My neighbors thought I was strange for taking walks, as if I was invading their privacy by choice. After my walk, I drove to work listening to the radio. Nelson Mandela had died the previous day. I can't remember if they said how. Old age, I think.

I worked at a health-food supermarket a few counties southward on the Bourbon Trail, between the Four Roses headquarters and the Wild Turkey distillery, in a flat town called Equus, where the gas stations were kept immaculate and horses outnumbered people. The drive was especially beautiful in the winter when long plains of perfect snow unsullied by red dirt and hoof prints and tractor tires blanketed the farmland in the early morning, lacing the edges of the salted interstate. At night, beneath the chalk-white bow of the crescent moon, shined the orbs of far-off suburban windows, and the sky was met with a faint blue dusting of hickory smoke.

The horses were kept in the stalls most of the season, making brief, listless appearances at the edge of the fence, and the cows grew a scrappy coating of dog fur and behaved no different than in the summer, grazing in uneven clusters or sitting alone in the most precarious and forlorn corner of the entire pasture with their legs curled beneath their girth. The police cars were boxy, angular. Time halted. In the summer, the pastures turned radiant green and the muscle-bound thoroughbreds triumphed against the daily commuters like me who passed the sides of the pastures like we were daring the horses to race. Some breeds could even outrun (if only for a short burst of victory) the reckless drivers from Ohio who traveled south for family reunions or whatever those disgusting people did with their time.

Each season went by and I forgot what the other looked like and marveled at the same benchmarks and oddities. When I lived in the city, new buildings appeared. Old ones were demolished. Whole blocks had been eaten up by pizza parlors, IPA pubs, and the hip new face of old yuppie gentrification. A fresh pink slip tucked into my coat (and most of the coats of my forgotten friends), I left the city still wondering where all the money had come from. It didn't matter because Equus, Bessemer, and Cantville never changed.

I took the same commute every day and listened to the same radio station and pulled into the parking lot exactly ten minutes before my shift began. In the winter I walked inside, hung up my coat, and poured myself a complimentary cup of coffee. In the spring I did the same. In the summer I drank maté throughout the workday to stay energized. I drank bourbon when I got home and turned on the television. Four Roses for paycheck weeks. Early Times when it wasn't. Just two short swigs to promote warmth in the stomach and head (then a few more for the rest of the limbs) and ease my thoughts.

My workday began with a long succession of "how are you doing?"s and "what's good?"s. I stepped through the deli kitchen to cut through to the grocery offices, running into every hairnet-wearing staff member I saw. The kitchen staff and deli attendants were the outlaws of the store; former chefs and restaurant workers from the upscale eateries of Chicago, Louisville, Indianapolis, and Knoxville who had either retired or abandoned the frantic pace of the to-order schedule for the lazy world of batch cooking for a health food store's cafeteria. I bought my weed from the kitchen people. There was one cook I remember in particular. Her name was Azalea. She was a forty-two-year-old white Jamaican woman who only stood five-feet tall in heels and weighed 120 pounds soaking wet. She had lived in Kentucky since her adolescence if not childhood and her accent was a mix of Patois and a terse Kentucky drawl. I talked to Azalea first even before Emanuel, who the store (or perhaps even Emanuel himself) had chosen to call E-man, or the manager, Todd, a short Polish kid from Florida, or Tommy, a tall dark guy from the meat department who had been a professional bluegrass musician and trucker across Appalachia in another life, or Willy in produce who always had something pithy up his sleeve and reeked of sweet Kentucky weed. Azalea was always the one I spoke to first and usually last. Her face, which was still by most standards objectively beautiful, displayed a distinctive wear-and-tear through dark creases in her subtly graying teeth and wrinkles in her face that tallied a few months lost to the hillbilly cocaine. She kept her hair wrapped in two Indian braids and matted down the rest of her scalp with a knitted cap. I remember a story she told Emanuel in the cold, dry air of the stocking room, a price gun in her hand.

"The doghouse," she said. "I'm about to go home to my doghouse."

"How come you in the doghouse?"

"I pissed him off again."

"Who you piss off?"

"Him."

"Him?"

"Okay, so I got a sense of humor that's rough around the edges. I know this. You know this."

"I heard that. What's going on with ya?"

"You know my husband used to be an alcoholic, right? I mean, him used to be a big mahn. But he just lost like thirty pounds An I think, he's alright with him weight, righ:? So we're jokin', just havin' a laugh. He play'd a prank on me for Valentine's Day. He say, 'I done got you a gift.' Shows me a computer page for a swingers website. I laugh. He laughs. Den he say, 'So for the day I could watch you screwin' a forty-year-old sack of flab. How's that sound?' I say, 'You want me tc put a mirror above our bed?' Then he get all incredulous about it. I tell him sorry, but he's still angry."

"You gotta make a gesture girl."

"All yesterday I'm gesturin'."

There were rumors that her husband still beat her from time to time. I never saw Azalea with a black eye or bruises. I'm not sure what her husband did for a living, but they had enough money to take a trip to Jamaica each winter. She'd disappear around February when the sky turned to smudges of coal ash. She would show me the pictures of the withered Kingston garrisons and the brightly painted storefronts, the clear ocean, and the crowded marinas. She had a bottle of Guinness in most of the pictures, the good kind with the yellow label that must have still tasted like something unlike the canned shit we import in the U.S. that's gone flat and tastes like aluminum. She looked forward to those February trips and said she was going back upon the rock. Jamaica was the rock. I would picture her lying on the beach in a white bikini, her strange, nimble body an oddity regardless of her surroundings, smoking a thick blunt. She smoked marijuana with the frequency of cigarettes, at least as far as I could tell in the uncomfortable atmosphere of the modern work environment. She was unfazed by the most potent strands. She bragged about smoking white-window in Zig-zag wrap. Despite her candid nature, she never admitted to her brief love affair with methamphetamine.

I drove Azalea home once. Her car had broken down in the parking lot and Tommy, the only guy with jumper cables, had gone home for the evening. She would have asked Emanuel for a ride but, as I had suspected sadly, women didn't trust him alone. I think she felt safer with me. I'm a timid guy. I'm a nice guy. I was already late when she asked and her ranch home wasn't very far. We drove in the darkness for a while, talking about other times we were in similar situations the way people do when they have nothing better to talk about. We got off the freeway and she told me to head down a long gravel road that passed by a trailer park I had seen on the news a few times because so much meth was cooked and sold there. Azalea said something about her best friend Julia living out there, and I seemed to recall a story she had told me about her. Julia worked as a masseuse in Cantville.

"Forty bucks for an hour-long session ain't bad," she said. "Especially not on a Saturday evening. Yeah, I'm headed out that way now. Gonna give her a nice tip for Christmas. She's excellent. Workin' for a new place now."

"A masseuse must be a good friend to have," I told her, stocking alkaline waters for Iceland.

"Oh, you bet. Got these three rowdy kids. One of 'em's a screamin' toddler. We hang out in her trailer a lot. So, the toddler comes up to us screamin'. She takes one touch on the shoulder, starts wiggling her thumb. The kid drops to the floor asleep like this..."

She fell to the floor to corroborate her story.

"She says, 'Damn, I'm good.' I say, 'You done knocked out your lil' pickney, geeyal!'"

We passed the trailer park and she muttered something else about Julia, then she told me to make a left at a scarecrow that almost made me jump in my seat. I looked like a demented hobo in the eerie glow of my headlights. The branch protruding from its sleeve could have been a rusted bread knife. Azalea's home was big and dark. Only one light was on in the kitchen. I could smell the smoke from the chimney in the car. I was envisioning her husband pulling her from my car with a bottle of whiskey in his hand, but the entire home appeared derelict except for the single kitchen light through which I could see a fridge decorated with photos and a wood-paneled hallway. She thanked me for the ride, gave me some cursory instructions on getting back and that was it.

That had been months before I found out she was fired. I was shocked when I found out the day after my dream. Tommy gossiped with me in the meat locker.

"One of the managers caught her taking a smoke break"-- Tommy lifted his fingers to form quotation marks-- "in her car before work."

"Aw, shit!" I said. "She got caught with weed?"

"No, it was a circular glass pipe."

"Jesus."

"Yeah," He paused. "She's got some issues."

I never saw her again. I worked a long day and drove home listening to a different radio station. The road was always empty at night except for a few trucks and wayward travelers heading up to Louisville or Indiana. I got home around 9: 40 pm. My headlights nearly touched my front door. I kept my keys in my hand when I got out of the car, but immediately noticed a slight aura of light around the perimeter of the door that told me it wasn't locked. My girlfriend was inside. She had a key to my place and seldom locked the door when she knew I'd be home so soon. I walked in and locked the door behind me. She was already on my couch in her pajamas.

"Hey, babe."

"Hey," I said.

"How was your day?"

I shrugged and said, "I had a weird dream just before I woke up."

"What about?"

"Hang-gliding."

"Bullshit."

I walked the three paces to the kitchenette. "Hey, can I have a glass of wine?"

"Sure."

I poured myself two fingers of bourbon and searched the cupboards for the glasses. I couldn't seem to find any since I never put anything back in the same place when I unload the dishwasher. I looked beneath the sink and found a dusty brass pail I once used for decoration in my old loft apartment, back when I lived in the city. It was the exact pitcher I gave to Willie Nelson. I ended up pouring my girlfriend her wine in a coffee mug. She took it and laughed, asking me if my other glasses were dirty. I told her it might be easier if I just left her a pitcher of wine. She laughed and lit a cigarette. I told her Azalea got fired and she nodded. I told her it was meth. She nodded again and tapped her ash into the crystal tray and told me to forget about it. We watched television for an hour or two and, when the news finally eclipsed the comedy shows, slumped along to the bedroom. I lay in bed thinking about vessels, listening to her breath in her sleep when I remembered the flowers in my dream home. The bushels of magenta blurred from my vision were azaleas. They had to be.

SHENANDOAH

My uncle killed himself after he returned to the continental United States. He hanged himself from the rafters of a gazebo on the Appalachian Trail with the rope I had given him from my dad's garage. He said he needed rope. Rope was the friend of the wilderness hiker. It was blue rope with red and yellow flecks; thin like bungee cord. I gave him all of it.

He said, "You always have to have good rope, you know?"

We had given him a ride to the Nantahala Valley in Cherokee country and turned him loose like a Cosmonaut. He had hiked the Sierra Nevadas and the Swiss Alps, smuggled money between East and West Germany in the eighties, and bicycled across America and Mexico. He sent us a postcard from the Shenandoah Valley before he died.

In Alaska, he slept in a national forest (the name of which I can't remember) until a group of black bears began to stalk his campsite. The forest rangers were incensed by the inconvenience and kicked him out of the park. He ended up working a grocery-store job in Anchorage and argued with bored teenagers in the dead of night. He was fired from that job, or left, and worked at a Taco Bell before the season changed when he spent the spring near Kodiak as a deckhand on a salmon boat. Once that job dried up, he landed an in-home hospice care position for an old Alaskan matriarch who'd taken close to eight years to die. Her son had converted a Jeep into a small bedroom for him, connecting it to an immense tube that funneled heat from the inside of the house. She died a month later. They celebrated her death immediately. Her suffering was over. Their lives were no longer stalled. Her spirit had left the body and they knew they had done the right thing all along, tending to her, loving her, keeping her as comfortable as they could even beyond their financial ability. They cooked steaks and bannock and cake and opened bottles of Vodka. My uncle drank with them in the kitchen, sitting quietly, preparing himself for homelessness.

He used to say the Alaskan deckhands were all on crack, crack, and meth. After Alaska, he lived with my grandparents back in Indiana for a little while. I went through his room while visiting a month before he died. He had letters from his daughter in the top drawer and underwear in the one below. Some of the underwear in the second drawer was soaked through with urine, fermenting in the Midwestern summer heat. I still don't know why, or what that might indicate.

He had spent time in a mental hospital shortly before we dropped him off at the Appalachian Trail. He mentioned being poked with a broom. He said they were trying to determine if he was violent.

The whispers of a serious life engaged in a sad hat trick of lonely misunderstanding and perforated eardrums continued. I was blind for some time. I didn't know what the experience meant to me. His death hurt me so much I never spoke to anyone. My family thought of me as a kind of sociopath. I was crass, unfeeling. But his death was something so unusual and close to me that it was sacred. To mention it was vanity or blasphemy. A callus had formed around it, a blanket of scar tissue that kept it safe. I shed no tears. I have never been genuine a day in my life with my family since the fifth grade.

My mother began to worry that our house was haunted. She saw my uncle in the corners of rooms. She followed his silhouette down the hall, half-believing it was my father. We heard footsteps inching across the carpet at night.

I think of him differently now. I see his spirit as an over-worked piston firing up and down within a corroding engine.

He first visited Alaska with my grandfather on vacation and decided not to leave. But where else was he going to go?

I want to know what his daughter thinks, but I imagine she has her own blanket of scar tissue that I can't anticipate or understand. Sometimes grief requires privacy; the privacy to perform the ritual of grieving. Some of us need to hold it close in the silence like a talisman. I had heard of a Baptist preacher's daughter in rural Oklahoma who lost her four-year-old son in a car accident and then immersed herself in an obscure, South Asian black magic. Photos of her middle-class, suburban home surfaced. Her walls were covered in hermetic symbols. The living room was taken over by a hand-made altar adorned in Sanskrit. My cousin lives in Brussels now. I don't know what she does for a living and I don't know how she thinks anymore.

My uncle, my cousin's father, my father's little brother, my grandfather's last son, was religious. He was evangelical in his alleged beliefs, which never made sense to me until I discovered that Kerouac was Catholic and suddenly it all made more sense than it ever really needed to. He did not write though, my uncle. He read voraciously, but he did not write unless it was to scribble criticisms and profanity in the margins of books he was reading. I read through a lot of them after his death. I found them by accident on my grandparents' bookshelf. He had underlined a sentence or a sentiment in *Catcher in the Rye* and wrote in the white space on the side of the page, "Are you kidding me?" He used to live in a converted farmhouse with my aunt and cousin. There was a stucco wall that surrounded the property. The original building felt like a homesteader's cabin from the 19th century. They had a cast-iron stove across from a modern fridge, a heavy wooden table, stairs that creaked and squealed which led to the vortex of the annexed sunroom, and a literal wall that had been converted into a bookshelf. There was a small room made from the converted shed for guests which they frequently rented out to travelers and tourists and possible vagrants. We took a walk in the rural landscape that surrounded his home with our dogs one Christmas and saw a stone alcove, a grotto of some sort shaped like the portion of a viaduct near the river. We went inside.

"This is a neat little installation," my dad said. "People come here to read or fish?"

"A bum might sleep in here at night," my uncle said.

He had a way of pulling the conversation into the darkness.

I still have the knife he gave me when he was drunk. The sunroom annex was full of people, all of them my aunt's friends. We were eating burnt goose and mashed potatoes infused with sour cream and vegetables the texture of bike-tire rubber, and an excess of jugged red wine. He sat down next to me on the couch in the interim between dinner and dessert and took out the folding knife. The wooden handle was deep maroon and the edges were gold. It was a Rough Rider jigged bone blade. In the old West, they called it a French tickler.

"You like this knife?"

"Yeah," I said.

"It's pretty cool," he said, unfolding the blade. "It's a good sharp blade, long. You see the little bee emblem when it locks into place right there?"

"Yeah."

"That's the old symbol of the French worker bee. The symbol of the Franc. If you ever get old enough and buy a bottle of Patrón tequila, you'll see the same symbol. It has to do with Napoleon III's attempted conquest of Mexico. Also, it's got a corkscrew right here in the handle. Very important."

I smiled and took in the Beaujolais fumes from his breath.

He handed me the knife.

"Merry Christmas."

Years later, my uncle stormed out of our house after a fight with his sister-in-law (not my mother) to smoke a cigarette on the lawn. I followed him outside with the cicadas chirping and stepped up behind him. He was angry and didn't want to look at me, didn't want me to be there, and I took out the knife he had given me to show him that I had kept it all this time.

"Hey hey, I remember that old knife," he said, the anger receding from his face

That night, he asked me to pull up a map on my computer so he could see the Pisgah National Forest and the Nantahala Valley. That's when he started devising his plan.

He gets up in the morning and sips coffee from an enameled cup over the coals of the fire and eats hard bread soaked in milk fat in the gray dawn of the Appalachian wilderness. I see him patching the hole in the tarpaulin over his tent to keep out the rain just to have something to do. His unwashed red hair shivers in the wind. His face is tired. There are bags under his eyes above the ginger stubble across his face. His supply of Schlitz malt liquor is gone as well as his dried apricots and beef jerky. He's lost days on the trail from gout in his toes. With no aspirin and no cherry juice, he has to take the pain. His brother gave him a bottle of Saint John's Wort before he left for depression. He has no cellphone; nowhere to go if he needs help. He sent out a postcard a week and a half ago. His hand trembled as he wrote it. He thought about saying goodbye. He thought about asking for help. But he's tired of taking things from everyone, from his parents, from his brothers, his sister-in-law. He used to have a house, a wife, a daughter, and a long series of short-term jobs. Some of them he seemed to care for. He worked on a road crew. He tended campsites at a state park. He had his plumber's certification. He enjoyed helping the Alaskan woman. He once had a life, or so it seemed to everyone around him. Not anymore. This trip isn't a hobby, it isn't a vacation. Everything he owns fits in his pack. He makes it to the night, trekking through the ominous woods by flashlight. The trail lets out into a parking lot and a long open field for dogs where he finds the gazebo. He considers hitch-hiking back home but doesn't. There is a small victory in his ability to tie the rope around the exposed rafter of the picnic gazebo. Holding the flashlight in his mouth, he gets the knot just right and grips the blue rope with both hands before lifting himself off the group to make sure it's sturdy enough to support his weight. The noose doesn't have to be perfect. It needs to be practical. He ties it one way, discards that method, and then wraps several lengths of the rope around his throat. He ties it off with a thick knot. He takes his last step off the edge of the two-by-four wooden rail.

I think of him when I write. I try to let him edit my work. I see his same comments in the margins: "Are you kidding me?"

I can't say I always liked him. Maybe I liked the idea of his adventures when I was younger and didn't know how, or what to express. That was before I knew how to express anything. And then I learned I couldn't express anything. What lesson do I have to teach? I don't. I'm just making music. I don't think my uncle ever appreciated Wittgenstein if he read him, and I'm sure he did. His internal feelings were better summed up by Kierkegaard. He was the kind of guy who thought everything had to have a point, everything needed to serve a purpose; a means to an end. That's why evangelical Christianity fit so well into his worldview. He took me to a basketball court once to get some exercise and would not allow me to play intuitively. He wanted perfect form from the layup every time. It was the same when we played badminton in the yard with my aunt. Everything had to be done a certain way, the right way. He played the same piano books from his childhood. This attitude didn't serve him well. My mother thought it came from a feeling of inferiority and shame since he never went to college. I think it's the reason he didn't go to college, or keep a job for too long. His thoughts were incompatible with the purposelessness of most things.

Of course, a wanderer's life is without purpose.

But I'm just making music.

Another hiker found him. My grandparents identified the body in Virginia. His ashes were buried in the family plot in Indiana. Nine years later, my grandfather was buried next to him, his youngest son.

I picked up some rust punks the other day and gave them a ride to the train depot. I loaded up their packs into the trunk and let them drink their bottle of Mad Dog in the backseat. They didn't care about my dirty car or the fact that I was a square. The three of them, two guys and a girl, were walking around the campus of a historically black college (they were all white) waiting to see if a famous chicken shack would throw out any drumsticks or breasts. I had just gotten off work and thought I'd give them a hand. They said they were headed north to Roanoke. I asked them about their travels and told them about my uncle and they didn't say much after that. I'm sure I came off kind of weird. We got to the train depot and I got out their packs and watched the three of them walk across the menagerie of track in the white-gravel dust toward a pink and dim orange sunset. They walked into the light and I was still there.

FRANKENSTEIN'S MONSTER

He could have been Frankenstein's monster from any horror film or regional theater production, no makeup, no latex required, she thought. He was only missing a tattered 19th-century frock coat to solidify the look.

She first saw him three months ago at the tail-end of the horrible summer. The manager and the stocker used to stand in the walk-in freezer on their off-time while she stood behind the register in the faint breeze of the window unit, sweating through her red polo shirt that had once belonged to her father. The stranger was nearly seven feet tall and had to crouch beneath the threshold as he entered the store. He bought standard poor-people things, staples: cans of beans, single pounds of only the discount ground beef, butter, milk, hot sauce, brown sugar, steel-cut oatmeal, eggs, and chocolate. He might have purchased beer, but Johnny's didn't have the cooler space for alcohol.

He had a genuine smile that revealed a massive congenital gap in his front teeth, a visible depression on the right side of his shaved scalp, moon-shaped scars under his eye sockets, and a large ridge on the left side of his face where a skin graft was evident. He came in close to every week since that first visit. She knew why. Despite the chain stores half a mile down the road killing their already meager business, Johnny's was never crowded. That meant no one was ever there long enough besides the three employees to stare at him. Wal-Mart must have been a nightmare for someone who looked like him.

He was a true stranger, not a trucker passing through or a lost tourist on their way to the beach. He had come to stay. He spoke with a Northern cadence, even punctuated his speech with 'eh' and 'ya know.' She didn't ask if he was foreign. He was not necessarily Canadian. He could have been from Wisconsin or Montana. She knew that much.

"The weather's gettin' real nice, eh?" he said, placing his things on the counter.

"It won't last."

"Nothin' ever does. It ever get cold down here?"

"Off and on through January and February," she said, running the cans across the weak scanner.

"How long you been here?"

"All my life."

"I meant the store."

"Long, long time," she said.

"You work here all your life too?"

Being a checkout clerk at Johnny's was not the kind of job you applied for. It was the kind of position you inherited through obligation. Murry, the owner, had bought the store from an expat Cuban-Chinese family in the late 70s with the life insurance money from his late wife. Forty years ago, his vision was to create a chain from the ground up like Publix. His current vision was to bulldoze the shack and sell the lot to a gas station. At first, Mickey (her name was Michaela, but she hated her name) had worked part-time throughout high school as a punishment for smoking weed in her bathroom. Her mother knew Murry's sister from a Christian book club and struck a deal. After losing her scholarship and dropping out of college, she returned to town and kept on working at Johnny's.

Who was Johnny? There was no Johnny, she thought. There was never a Johnny.

She had locked up for the evening about ten minutes early. Dale and Murry were long gone and already drunk. With her black apron still on, she sat on the wooden front steps and lit a cigarette. The sound of heavy footfalls on loose gravel inched toward her and she saw Frankenstein's monster emerge from the wild bamboo and rhododendrons in the dusk afterglow. She took a drag on the cigarette, half startled.

"We're closed," she said.

"That's fine. I don't need anything."

He was about to turn around.

"Hey," she said. "Where are you from?"

"Where am I from?"

"Yeah."

"I'm from Ontario."

"You're Canadian?"

"Yep."

"What are you doing down here?"

He chuckled.

"Stuff," he said.

That night, she headed west on the single-lane road to the abandoned elementary grounds where her favorite redbrick courtyard was hidden in bushels of dying elephant grass and gates of twisted iron. Raccoons moved through the canopy of dense palmetto leaves above the clustered trees, scrapping the gutter that lined the edge of the ancient rooftop. There was some graffiti around the shattered windows. It was old and faded. Blast marks from New Year's mortars spread across the corroded brick in opaque dream-like patterns. Tera used to meet her here with a six-pack of Smirnoff Ice and a blunt. But Tera was long gone; a different college, a different life. Knowing her, she was probably drowning in pussy; hairy hippie cunts that capture their moisture just right beneath those peasant skirts she had once thought about wearing. Her life was probably full of magic mushrooms and chakras and tantric threesomes in the Appalachian wilderness. And Mickey was still here. No more clandestine fingerings in the dead of night. No more half-enlightened discussions on feminism. What was she gonna do in this town? She had a chance at a small college on the coast thirty minutes away, but she blew it. Years from now, Tera will start commuting to her creative job in a metropolitan city center, and Mickey will be a fat old dyke who sacks groceries for a living.

She sat down by the dried-up fountain. A thick, black rat snake slithered between her feet toward the bushes. She smoked a cigarette and listened to the chattering of the raccoons.

She liked to watch internet videos of monkeys grooming one another before she fell asleep. That or a video of a British ergonomist explaining the correct posture for sitting at the computer. She speaks softly but the audio is sensitive enough it almost picks up the saliva building upon her tongue, between her teeth. The young woman in running clothes that she uses as a model sits and stands, lets her caress her back as she talks about her spine, and pivots her neck as she places her fingers on the hinges of her jaw. It's all vaguely sapphic. The monkeys were just monkeys. Monkeys were funny to her. She also felt comforted by the insinuation of their sophisticated social order.

She fell asleep in her childhood bed flanked on both sides by fixtures of a life she had tried and failed to escape: a cross on the far wall and her old dresser with her baby changing station built into a folding compartment on top.

She woke up in the middle of the night and heard rustling downstairs. The floorboards squealed. Plates crashed into one another. It didn't sound like her mother. Her mother was a ghost. She got out of bed and took the Winchester off the wall mount in the hallway. It was always empty, but it looked intimidating. She walked down the carpeted steps. The noises were getting louder: the sound of a bag being torn open followed by chewing. Turning the corner, she aimed the barrel in front of her and racked the lever to indicate she had chambered a cartridge. The possum stared back at her with its beady eyes as it nibbled on the dried bread crust from the open garbage bag. She lowered the rifle and sighed. Her mother had left the window open above the sink to save on AC, and the little bastard had exploited a minor tear in the screen. She opened the back door and swept him away with the stock, poking at his patchy gray fur as he waddled down the steps into the bull thistles.

"Be free," she said, "Be free, you fearless beast."

The hefty critter scaled the aluminum fence across the field and raced along the knuckled selvage to a low-hanging oak branch. He was gone.

She closed the window and set the loose dishes the possum had miraculously not shattered back into the sink the locked the back door. The moon was low in a strange clear sky. She set the Winchester in the corner and crouched to her knees to clean up the wadded napkins and bits of food strewn across the floor.

She used to help her mother hand out religious comics at Halloween instead of candy. Most kids didn't have a problem with that in this town. The trick-or-treaters around here were members of the same church. Halloween candy wasn't something she nor her peers longed for. The high-fat, high-sodium, high-sugar diet of frequent church potlucks was enough. Gluttony didn't strike her as a Baptist sin. She supposed (and she could only infer this from movies and a cursory knowledge of the Northeast) it was the same for Catholics and drinking. She didn't know what a eucharist was until she went to an Episcopal church near the college campus. And she only went one Sunday in October because of the pride flags hanging from the columns of the portico. One year, right at the eve of her adolescence, she handed out some Jack Chick cartoons to a group of kids she hadn't seen before at school or church. Their house was egged later that night. The next day she was cleaning the yard and hosing down the vinyl siding when she saw the rectangular booklets tossed into the bushes. She fished them out from under the loquat and, sitting in the yard with the running hose by her side, gave the cartoons an honest read. A strange thing happened. She laughed. She laughed her ass off. These stupid comics she had been handing out for so long weren't teaching anyone anything. They weren't changing minds or helping to assuage doubt. They weren't even kind. These little booklets of black and white illustrated scenarios were just awful. She laughed. She had to laugh. She laughed at the gay guys converting the world's male population to gayness; the Muslim extremist who accepts Allah is just moon-god trickster and converts two pages later; the theologian who burns in hell for admitting other religions have merit. She threw them in the garbage with the eggshells.

In the morning, she walked into the kitchen and her mother was opening a fresh box of church fliers and Jack Chick comics for the upcoming fundraiser.

"Why was the air-conditioning on all night long?"

"Because it's hot," she said, grabbing a cold bottle of water from the fridge.

"Why weren't the windows open?"

"They were, and then I closed them. A possum got inside the kitchen and opened up our trash."

"Oh, you're so full of it. You know I have to pay for that air-conditioning. Leave it on all night and it racks the bill up like crazy. We're in winter now. It gets cold at night."

"It doesn't get cold here, Mom. It never gets cold here."

"I'm sure you think it's some kind of global warming BS."

She drank half the bottle of ice-cold water and sat down at the table. She said nothing.

Her mother stuffed an equal amount of fliers and Chick tracts into a series of manilla envelopes labeled with the volunteer's names.

"Mom?" Mickey said, breaking a long silence.

"What?"

"Why did you bother to write everyone's name down if each packet has the same stuff?"

She paused.

"They're not all the same," she said.

"They look the same."

"Well, they're not."

She finished her water.

Her mother stuffed the last envelope and moved the giant stack over to a plastic bin by the sink. She noticed the possum-sized gash in the window screen and sighed.

"Oh, Mickey. I'm sorry. You weren't kidding, were you?"

Mickey shook her head in silence.

"Now I feel bad. I'll have to replace that now. Shit!"

"Life is life, eh?" she said, mimicking a Canadian accent.

Her mother froze.

"What did you say?"

"Life is life."

"Are you tryin' to lose your accent now?"

"I'm just having fun. You know this guy's been shopping at Johnny's a lot lately. He's from Canada."

"Canada? What the hell is he doing down here?"

Mickey laughed.

"Stuff," she said.

Frankenstein's monster did not appear for an entire week. Their business was slow enough that his absence was noticeable. They had their regulars: an old guy in a cowboy hat who loaded his truck with sacks of cornmeal, another even older guy who sat and drank Ne-Hi grape soda on the porch for hours, and a group of Mexican road workers who bought supplies for lunch as well as the long drive home further inland.

The next week, her mom had to take the car for an evening church function. She dropped her off at Johnny's and the idea was for her to walk home.

"That's how young girls go missing, Mom."

"Don't you make me feel bad about this."

She locked up early again (there wouldn't be any customers after five-thirty) when Murry and Dale split for the local bar. She sat on the porch in the evening breeze with a Coca-cola she hadn't paid for and ignited a joint instead of a cigarette. She smoked and sipped the drink. The wind rustled the rhododendron leaves and swayed the thin pines. Their trunks groaned like tightening rope. The palmettos were unmoving except for their tassel-shaped leaves juxtaposed against the red horizon like mutated dandelions.

"This place sucks," she said out loud.

"I don't know. I kind of like it."

She jumped two feet to the left and spilled part of the Coca-cola.

The Canadian was standing beneath her on the porch, his hand on the two-by-four railing, watching the sun get low.

"The hell, dude?"

"Sorry, I thought you saw me."

"No!"

"Sorry. Are you guys closing early now?"

She caught her breath.

"Yeah, no. Kind of. What do you need?"

He sniffed the air.

"You smokin' weed?"

"No, it's a cigarette."

"Can I get a hit?"

She hesitated.

"Yeah, just don't tell nobody."

She passed him the joint.

He took a small hit and immediately started coughing.

"It's been a while," he said, passing it back.

"It's not great stuff."

"It'll do."

"I can open up the register if you need to grab something right quick."

"I don't need anything," he said, "What do you do for fun around here?"

She raised the burning joint as the remnants of a stem sizzled on the ember like a sprig of dry sassafras.

"We make our own fun."

"You folks don't have a movie theater or a steakhouse…"

"Nearest movie theater is a half-hour away on the island."

"Yeah, but what else do people do, you know?"

"They go to church, or they develop a drinking problem."

He laughed.

"Where I come from the two aren't mutually exclusive, eh."

She took a drag on the joint and blew into the wind, letting it carry the smell away.

"Where exactly are you from? I mean like in Ontario."

"Oh, you remember me telling you that."

He shifted his feet as he leaned against the rail.

"Truth be told," he said, "I'm from Norway House, Manitoba. But I grew up and lived all my life in London, Ontario."

"Ontario has a London?"

"Yep," he said.

"Why are you in the States now? And why not Ohio or somewhere nicer."

"You don't like it here?"

"Of course, I don't."

"I don't mind it here. It doesn't get cold."

"What do you do for a living?"

"Nothing right now," he said.

"You don't work?"

"I live off a settlement. Employer negligence. That's why my face is like this."

"What happened?"

"Industrial accident. I worked in a sugar factory. Things weren't up to code. I don't like to relive it."

"That's fine," she said, offering him the joint.

He took another hit, deeper this time, and exhaled an even stream of white smoke.

"Why don't you go down to the beach to spend your settlement money? What's so great about this little town anyway?"

"There's nothing particularly special about this town. I've just been looking for somebody and they happen to live here."

She stamped out the joint on a nearby beam and set what was left in her cigarette pack.

"Who's that?"

"My daughter."

"Really?"

He nodded.

"What's her name?"

"Michaela. But she goes by Mickey."

"That's not funny."

"I'm not trying to be funny."

"You're not my dad," she said.

"I'm pretty sure I am. I left Eleanor back in 1992. That'd make you 19 years old?"

"I'm 20."

"I wasn't that far off then."

"Fuck off, asshole."

She jumped down the wooden steps and started down the road toward her house.

He didn't follow her. He stood there in the ankle-high crabgrass and watched her slowly disappear around the lone bend on the country road. He shook his head. The sun crashed into the treeline as shadows stretched over Johnny's. The air chilled. He turned back toward the bamboo and walked along the trail. Surrounded by forest, he crossed the leafy gulch and took long, practiced strides to avoid the razor-like brambles. His tent was covered in a blue tarp and, on the same string tied between two lines, his clothes dried in the salty air. He had his portable gas stove, his pot, and pan, an enameled coffee pot. He sat down on the fibrous, coarse palmetto stump and rubbed his knees. He sat until dark and then crawled back inside his tent.

ABOUT THE AUTHOR

Connor de Bruler was born in Indiana and grew up in Germany and South Carolina. He lives in Columbia, South Carolina.